TYREE

Book Three in the Galaxy Gladiators Alien Abduction Romance Series

Alana Khan

Temptation of the Horizontal Publishing, LLC

Copyright

Contents

Prologue

PRESENT DAY

Somewhere in space on the bridge of the spaceship *Sweet Deliverance*

23 days ago

Grace

Tyree's handsome face thrashes against the pillow of his hospital bed as he tosses and turns in agony. Sometimes he just lies there, completely out of it and comatose, but for the past hour he's been restless. He's shifting wildly under his covers, moaning in pain and talking gibberish. My subdural translator is having trouble deciphering his words—maybe because they're only fragments. Whatever he's saying, he sounds frantic and terrified.

I smooth a wet washcloth over his forehead, trying to calm him.

"It's okay, Tyree. It will be alright," I croon. But I'm lying. I've watched him over the last few days, and he doesn't seem to be getting any better. If anything, he gets weaker and less tied to reality with every passing hour.

He groans again. His exposed arms over the covers are cramping so tightly I can actually see the muscles spasm under his skin. My God, he must be in excruciating pain.

I glance at the readout above his head. I'm no nurse, but Dr. Drayke taught me how to decipher the numbers. His temperature's spiked again.

"Medbot, administer four *ligulas* of Tri-cam Nine," I instruct, just like the doctor taught me.

But the meds don't seem to help. Nothing seems to help. The doctor's twenty feet away in his adjoining lab, up late again tonight, scouring the Intergalactic Database looking for a cure.

A little over two weeks ago myself and nine other females were kidnapped from Earth and brought aboard this spaceship as breeding stock. We were each chipped with a subdural translator, placed in a pain/kill slave collar, and thrown into a cell with an alien gladiator. I didn't yet know my cellmate's name when we were forced to mate under threat of death. Shadow was physically harsh and emotionally distant.

One week later we overthrew our captors and took over this ship. Getting my own cabin and not having to interact with Shadow was a huge relief. It was only then that I began to come to terms with the fact that I'd never see Earth again.

Tyree and I became friends after the insurrection. He was three feet tall and non-threatening. I was comfortable with him, and despite the fact we were from different planets, it felt like we'd known each other for years. He wasn't just small, we all thought of "him" as "her." We now know he didn't have a gender.

Two days ago with no warning, he transformed into the huge, muscular alien lying on the bed in front of me. I imagine his declining condition is the result of the stress on his system from morphing in the span of half an hour from a Keebler elf to Dwayne "The Rock" Johnson.

In the few days between our escape and his illness, he and I had been building a friendship. In fact, we had a couple "sleepovers" when we watched vids together in bed and played a gambling game he taught me. I felt closer to Tyree than anyone on board.

I've been watching him 24/7 in this medbay since his change—I haven't left his side. I want to make certain his vitals don't crash if the doctor is preoccupied or leaves for a moment.

I've learned some basics on how to care for him. Dr. Drayke can't be here constantly, but I can. I have no nursing training, but keeping his brow sponged and filling his feeding reservoir with nutri-food isn't rocket science.

Tyree settles for a moment, his massive body quiet and still. This scares me as much as when he's thrashing. I glance at his vitals on the screen. His blood pressure is approaching the dangerously low numbers that indicate he'll need a shot of adramine. The doc taught me how to administer that, too.

With one eye on the medscreen, I pick up my instrument. I bought it recently on planet Numa and dubbed it "String Thing." My music is the only thing that seems to calm him.

Since we won our freedom, new tunes flow out of my fingers almost without effort. At this moment, I improvise a lilting melody that sounds like an ancient Irish folk tune. It makes me picture happy people converging toward a medieval fair. The chords are festive and inviting.

This seems to have a calming effect on Tyree, and his huge frame relaxes, the tense muscles in his face loosen. I stop playing long enough to smooth his sheets and tuck them around him. He grabs my hand, opens his luminous emerald eyes, and pierces me with a penetrating stare.

"Grace," his voice is no louder than a sigh. Then he closes his lids, groans, and flails his arms.

His violent movements heave the covers off his bed and onto the floor. I reach over to pull the bedrails up before he falls.

"Doc!" I call, but he doesn't answer. Maybe he hurried to his cabin for a quick nap.

Tyree's now back in his unconscious state, so I bend to retrieve the sheets, then turn to cover him. I'm caught off guard by his nude, flawless, masculine body. I'm paralyzed in mid-motion. How could any being possess such perfection?

I quickly cover him, pulling the sheets all the way up under his chin. But the image I just glimpsed is now burned into my brain. I picture him from tousled blond hair to strong brow, to aquiline nose. His lips are full and inviting. The lean muscles sculpted under his skin belong on the statue of a Greek god.

My mouth is parched just from that brief flash of bronze flesh and hard muscle. I position his arms on top of the blanket and smooth a nonexistent wrinkle. Why do my fingers itch to trace the strong veins that run from inner elbow to wrist?

I finally force myself back to my chair, grab String Thing, and return to my music. But this isn't the happy tune that could be played at a Renaissance county fair. This is a tune of longing—a woman pining for a lover who was conscripted and forced to march off to war. A woman who desires her man.

No one knows I was a virgin when I was thrown into a cell and forced to mate. A virgin by choice. I've never considered myself a sexual being. At twenty-five, I was very comfortable with the idea of being single forever. But right now, this minute, I question that decision with every fiber of my being. Because this alien male who I was becoming friends with awakens feelings in me I've never had before. There's a deep, long-hidden part of me that wants to be more than friends. Much more.

Chapter One

GRACE

As I hurry to the bridge at Captain Zar's request, I don't know why my thoughts have turned to that day three weeks ago when I was caring for Tyree. Those were dark days when we all feared he would die. Thankfully, Shadow cured him through their psychic connection a few days later.

It's hard to even think how close to death Tyree was, how worried I was for him. Now he's healthy and putting on even more muscle every day. He's happy and seems to be figuring out how to step into his new role. He's even training to help pilot this vessel.

"Thanks for coming, Grace. I have great news," Captain Zar excitedly greets me as I step through the doors to the bridge.

I take a moment to glimpse out the expansive floor-to-ceiling windows that encircle most of the bullet-shaped room. In the weeks since we fought for our freedom I've come to love this view.

I glance at the endless array of stars and purple nebulae in the vast expanse of velvet black space. It usually relaxes me, but I'm on high alert because Zar's never called me to the bridge before and despite his upbeat words, my naturally paranoid self is thinking whatever's coming can't be good.

Zar beams at me expectantly. I usually enjoy his calm strength, having learned weeks ago how to ignore our physical differences—he's a huge feline humanoid. Tyree's sitting casually in his first mate's chair, his ankle crossed over his knee. Between his handsome face and what's almost hanging out of his well-packed loincloth, I feel awkward under his warm gaze. I've been avoiding him lately—as attracted as I am to him, his obvious masculine interest makes me nervous.

"Sit down, Grace," Zar motions me into the empty seat at the comms panel, then sits in his wide captain's chair.

"You must be wondering why I called you here. Were you aware that Callista got bored one night at her comms post and put your music out over the Intergalactic Database?"

I shake my head, not even sure what to do with this piece of information, and certainly not sure why this is such "great news."

"She told me to tell you...let me check my notes...she put your 'greatest hits' on a channel that 'went viral.' I'm not sure what that means. Do you understand?"

"Kind of," I hedge even as my mind starts quickly calculating possible catastrophic outcomes that might result from this information.

"She said millions of beings heard it and began sharing it with others and giving it accolades."

"Okaaay." My spidey senses tell me something's coming that I'm not going to like. My stomach clenches and my palms start to sweat.

"In addition to all sorts of messages praising your music and your performance, you also received an invitation to play on planet Emirus—from the Emperor himself." He's grinning at me. His golden feline features look more fearsome than happy with his face lifted in a smile, possibly because of the inch-long canines peeking out beneath his cat-like lips.

"They're going to pay you three hundred thousand credits! Just to sit in a beautiful dress on a fancy stage in a huge symphony hall, and play the music you've already composed.

This is a fantastic opportunity for us all. It will keep us in fuel and much-needed mechanical updates for an entire lunar cycle. What a lucky break."

There are twenty-three souls on board this vessel. In the last weeks since we overthrew our slave masters and commandeered this ship, we've been roaming the underbelly of the galaxy. Our males have been making money in gladiatorial matches—some state-sponsored, some in sketchy underground venues.

It's been clear since the beginning of our adventure that credits are in short supply, but this? My hands begin trembling.

"Lucky break," I repeat Zar's words dully. My mind finally catches up with what he just told me and now it's not just my hands that are quaking—anxious tremors are shooting through my entire body.

"A two-hour concert on three consecutive days," Tyree chimes in happily. "Those three concerts will net more credits than ten gladiator matches. And no one has to risk their life!" He spears me with a proud, encouraging look.

My traitorous body responds before my thoughts catch up. I'm nauseous, complete with a rumble and tightness in my belly. I press the soles of my feet to the floor in an effort to counteract the dizziness that's making the room spin. Gripping the arms of my chair, I try to stay put as I order my body to stand down, but I soon realize the nausea is more powerful than I am.

I bolt out of my chair with no explanation. My lips are tightly clamped to make sure I don't hurl in front of my shipmates. Running down the hall to the nearest restroom, I try to choke back the acid making its fiery climb up my throat and threatening to propel out of my mouth.

After gargling, I splash cool water on my cheeks. I don't like the face in the mirror that's looking back at me. My eyes are wide and shiny and full of fear. I'm not this person. I have inner strength. I've been in jams before. I lived through kidnap and a bloody insurrection. I can power my way through this.

But I can't, a weak, whiney voice in my head insists. I've had a physical reaction to performing since my first recital. Every music teacher I've ever had praised me and told me I was destined to play in front of audiences. But I became a barista instead—I'm not built to perform. When I play in front of people my body reacts as if I'm in a war zone. I've gone to therapy, taken meds, had sessions of hypnosis—it never made a dent in this anxiety.

Panic. For some people it's thunder, for others it's heights or spiders, for me it's performing. My body makes an end-run around my mind and reacts like this!

Did Zar say "huge symphony hall"? Really? With just that thought, I heave, missing the toilet and splattering all over the sink and metal walls. Crap!

While I'm cleaning up I do all sorts of positive self-talk and calming breaths, and even some crazy tapping technique therapist number three taught me. My stomach is still rumbling, and hot waves of nausea are flowing through me.

Finally, my gut settles, I'm breathing normally, and the walls are clean—although the bathroom definitely needs to be fumigated.

I think of all the reasons my shipmates need me to perform. We're now in possession of this ship but no money. Even though some of the gladiators have fought on various planets to make income, credits are still in short supply. And our former owners, the MarZan cartel, are pursuing us. Not only do they still consider us their "property"—they want their ship back. They've advertised a hefty price on our heads to every slaver, pirate, and crook in the galaxy.

"Grace," I order the pale, wide-eyed face looking out at me from the mirror, "you're going to walk back on that bridge and agree to do it. Every person on this ship will benefit from this. You will figure this out—you have to. Every life on board depends on it."

After one more splash of water, I throw my shoulders back, lift my chin, and drag my feet back to the bridge with as much dignity as I can muster. The room is quiet, with that "oh no, we weren't talking about you" vibe as I enter the double doors.

"I'll do it," my voice is strong with false bravado. "I'll figure it out." I've survived worse.

The relief on their faces is palpable.

"I have an idea," Tyree interjects. "You know what I did before the overthrow, right?"

Yes, I certainly know what he did, we've talked about it many times. But right now my brain freeze is so severe all I can do is raise a questioning eyebrow because my mind can't find the answer to his question.

"I calmed the previous captain. That was my job as a slave. I sat at his feet right there," he points at the floor near Zar's chair, "and used my psychic powers to reduce his anxiety. I lay at the foot of his bed every night and calmed him to sleep.

"That was before my Transformation. Since then, my powers have increased." He spears me with his blazing, emerald gaze. "I could do that for you, Grace. We could begin as soon as you'd like. I can relax you, ease your fears. I can help you get through this."

He just threw me the only lifeline I'm going to get.

"Thanks, Tyree. That's generous. I'll take you up on your offer. Can we meet tomorrow at breakfast?"

Tyree

Grace has such a strong effect on me I usually try to avoid her. And now I've promised to meet her tomorrow morning? Right now I'll embarrass myself if I don't figure out a way to sneak to the restroom to rearrange my cock in my loincloth.

Why did I offer to spend time alone with her? Stupid question. First, she obviously needs help. Second, it gets me increased access to her—both of us in a room, alone, with no intruders. I crave it and dread it in equal measures.

Ever since my Transformation, I spring erections at least five times a day, usually more. My friend Shadow says I'm going through adolescence even though I'm thirty-five. Whether I'm fifteen or thirty-five, these feelings are overwhelming and all-consuming.

Hustling into the private bathroom in my cabin, I begin what is my most frequent pastime as of late. I practically rip off my loincloth and grab my cock. I've read that most people use many different fantasies when they touch themselves. I only have one. Grace.

I visualize her from head to toe. I imagine her shoulder-length blond hair and her large blue eyes—they remind me of the sky on my home planet of Larian. I appreciate that she often wears pretty dresses that accentuate her femininity. I picture the way she walks, so graceful and delicate without trying to call attention to herself.

But my thoughts are pulled to the sensations my hand is producing. In my mind, it's not *my* hand that's caressing me, but Grace's small, soft, nimble one. Closing my eyes, I feel her slim, cool fingers discovering me, exploring from base to tip and back. My engorged cock throbs in time with my swiftly-beating heart. My blood is like hot lava coursing through my veins.

I picture her nude body, pink-tipped breasts swaying as she works me. I imagine the smell of her arousal.

I'm so close to release I skip to the best part of my fantasy—when her knees slowly descend to the floor, her eyes never leaving mine. She sensually licks her lips, and her warm mouth surrounds my cock.

It's the labor of a moment, working myself hard, manhandling myself, before I spurt into the toilet. I immediately flush the evidence down the drain before my heart rate returns to normal.

Part of me wants to bask in the physical release, the calm bliss of the aftermath of my orgasm, but I don't allow it. I'm still not used to these base needs. I lived thirty-five *annums* without them. I resent them.

I step to the sink to wash any remnants from my hands and cock. As I dry myself with a towel, I catch my reflection in the mirror. Shaggy golden hair, glowing green eyes, strong jaw. I still see a stranger when I glance at my reflection.

It was less than two lunar cycles ago when I examined myself in a mirror just like this in the room I shared with the captain. I was only three *fiertos* tall, so I had to jump up on the sink, my knobby little knees perched on each side of the cabinet, so I could peer at my reflection.

That was the exact moment I realized the Transformation was coming. My round, cherubic face was manifesting harder planes and angles. I observed defined muscles in my calves for the first time in my life.

I was abducted by slavers from my home planet at the age of seven. I had only recently learned about the Transformation. Larians are born sexless, or as Dr. Drayke explained, intersexed. I had two vents between my legs for excretion.

Some of my race never transform. Others do—but only when they've met their truemate.

I still don't understand how it happens. Dr. Drayke says he can find nothing in the literature. My planet was so backward, there was no research available about my homeworld. Two Larians would meet and for some reason, it would trigger the Transformation. One would become male and the other female. Then they'd celebrate with a mating ceremony, and later, perhaps offspring.

I figured I'd be this odd, sexless, tiny person forever because I would never meet another Larian. And certainly never Transform.

Now here I am, stooping a little to catch a good look in the mirror. If I glimpse myself when I'm in the right frame of mind, I can see what the others on the ship see when they view me: a tall, powerful male with broad shoulders, strong muscles, and observant green eyes. But most of the time I still think of myself as I've been most of my life: short, slight, and weak.

But when I'm near Grace I never feel that way. I can't forget I'm all male when I'm around her. I'm protective of her, wanting to keep her away from the other males. I want to get to know her better and learn every memory, good or bad, that made her into who she is today.

I want to take care of her, provide for her, and bring food to her. When we eat together I have to tamp down my urge to feed the best morsels to her—I know she'd hate me doing that in front of our friends.

It's not just my body and emotions that have changed since my Transformation. I haven't admitted to anyone how much my psychic powers have increased. Before, I could only enter someone's mind when they invited me. About the only thing I could do was calm them, which is what kept me alive through all my *annums* as a slave.

Now my gift is more powerful, I can occasionally catch words or phrases drifting from my shipmates' minds as I sit next to them or pass them in the hall.

It's a blessing Grace's thoughts never stray into my own. I find it calming to be in her presence. Between the lack of mind chatter and her sweet soul, there's no one on board I'd rather spend time with.

Except for the erections. Those are worse when she's around. And now I've offered to spend more time with her until her concert commitment is fulfilled.

Chapter Two

I ate dinner alone in my room; I just couldn't bear to be around other people tonight. They'll be laughing and joking, and I'll just be a bundle of self-absorbed nerves. I don't want to be pathetic or needy, I'd rather be alone.

Although I've been out of captivity and safely ensconced in this cabin for over a month, it feels cold and foreign. The twelve-by-twelve space has dull metal walls, a double bed, dresser, tiny corner desk, and a chair. It connects to a utilitarian private bathroom. I haven't had the time, money, or opportunity to do anything to it. There isn't one personal item in here—except for my instruments.

I have two: String Thing, which I bought on planet Numa, and an electronic multi-purpose instrument I found in the abandoned wing of the ship. Composing and playing my music are the only pastimes that soothe me.

Now, with this horrible series of concerts looming over me, my music is a double-edged sword. It calms me for a moment, then fills me with dread when I contemplate playing in front of a concert hall full of people.

Even though I only have twenty shipmates, it's a miracle I've played for them twice since we took over the ship. I feel so comfortable and close to my new friends I somehow found the courage to perform for them.

The first time it gave everyone the opportunity to dance with their former cellmates—and gave me an excuse to not have to dance at all. There was a lot of romance in the air that night, and no one was focused on me or my music, just their partner. The second performance was to honor Tyree's Transformation in the only way I knew how—the gift of music. My stomach was in knots playing just that one piece for everyone, but I forced myself to do it—for him.

Tonight is dragging by. The hundredth time I glance at the clock, I'm relieved to see it's time for bed. Of course, sleep chooses to elude me. Instead, my thoughts keep looping back to my first recital.

Mom was there with her boyfriend du jour. Actually, this one stuck around longer than most. Too bad, because he was one of the meanest of all the men who lived with us for a while when they were down on their luck or too lazy to work.

I remember he told me to call him Candyman. It wasn't until I was much older that I realized how inappropriate it was for a second grader to be calling her mom's drug dealer Candyman.

I've watched this particular memory so many times I push fast forward in my mind. I gloss over the details and just remember his vicious comments on the car ride home from the recital.

"You're stupid. An idiot. You made a fool of yourself," his voice was derisive. "You think the audience clapped because they liked it? They just didn't want to hurt your feelings. But I heard them laughing at you while you played. The woman in front of us told her husband she'd never heard anything so terrible. You played it all wrong. Made a dozen mistakes. Right, Terese?"

I'll never forget mom's head bobbing up and down in the front seat, agreeing with him. I'll also never forget the beating I got when we arrived home. First, he used his hand, then his belt. That was the first and last time I performed comfortably in public.

My hands are slick with sweat, my teeth clamped shut in tension, and my heart aches in sympathy for my younger self.

Hours later, I've watched a parade of reruns of Candyman's relentless ridicule and putdowns. After living with his harsh contempt for a few years it's a wonder I have a shred of self-esteem left.

I'm bathed in a cold sweat just thinking about my upcoming concert. It doesn't matter that half the galaxy loves my music—tell that to my antiquated "lizard brain"—it's on high alert as if I'm in the middle of a battlefield.

I concede that lying here is futile; the anxiety is just too compelling. I head to my bathroom, then slip under the shower for a moment to rinse off the sweat. Why did I arrange to meet up with Tyree tomorrow morning? I should have known I'd need his help tonight.

After getting dressed, I wander through the ship's narrow, metal hallways for a while, but I knew where I was heading when I left my cabin—the bridge—to see Tyree.

"Come in. Can't sleep?" Tyree offers, concern in his warm voice. I thought Axxios, the huge, golden pilot, might be here with him, but it's just Tyree and me in this quiet, enclosed space.

He knows me pretty well. We shared a lot those few days before his Transformation. I'll be honest, I've done my best to avoid him since he recovered. My mouth goes dry every time I remember the image of him in bed with his sheet pooled on the floor. And my traitorous mind throws that picture at me far too frequently. I liked him better before he became this huge, masculine Adonis. I was more comfortable.

"You're right, Tyree, I can't sleep. But I know you're busy..." It was foolish to come. I know he has work to do, I don't want to be selfish. But instead of leaving, I sit at the comms desk behind Tyree who's in the captain's chair.

Axxios, the pilot, has been giving Tyree lessons at the helm. We need more than one person who can drive this ship. Tyree flies this vessel alone at night when Axxios leaves to catch some sleep.

"So, you've been given the go-ahead to pilot this thing? You must be a fast learner," I look at the panel in front of him filled with incomprehensible buttons, levers, and switches as well as several glowing, blinking computer screens.

"I know how to keep us on the course Axxios sets. With a little coaching, I can set new coordinates, but I'm much slower than Axx."

I glance out the floor-to-ceiling windows. The view is spectacular from here—as it should be since this is command central for the ship. I try to let the endless stars in the sky calm me.

Tyree is turned to face me, so I'm the only one gazing out the bank of windows. My eyes open wide in fear—a ship just appeared out of nowhere in front of us.

Perhaps it's the look of abject terror that crosses my face, but Tyree's head swiftly pivots to where I'm looking. He immediately launches into high gear.

"Taking evasive maneuvers!" he shouts, his fingers flying on his computer. "*Drack*, that device was cloaked. My panel gave no warning. Computer, call Axxios to the bridge. Now!"

A ten-foot-tall face appears on every other one of the floor-to-ceiling windows that double as communication vid screens at the prow of the ship. "Your call letters identify as the *Sweet Deliverance*," the hideous face announces. The male is spotted in ugly, amphibious shades of brown with spikes protruding from his forehead, brow ridges, and chin.

"Gren," Tyree breathes.

Crap! Our former captain. We knocked him out and released him on planet Numa after the overthrow. He's a minion for the MarZan cartel.

"Funny, I could swear this ship is the *Warbird One*, owned by the MarZan cartel," his voice is condescending and provocative. "We've come to collect our property."

Our ship veers sharply, the engine making one loud, grinding noise that doesn't inspire confidence. Where's Axxios?

"You're sitting ducks out here," Gren taunts. "This should be fun."

I see a laser burst barreling toward us and I brace for impact. The ship lurches, but it's a near miss. The corners of Gren's mouth turn up in evil glee.

"Just wait, things will get worse." He's toying with us.

"I'm trying to outrun him, but his ship's better equipped," Tyree's voice is tight.

We speed up, taking evasive maneuvers, Tyree's kicked us into high gear. He's competently zigzagging to dodge Gren, but the other ship is hot on our tail.

"How do I hail him back, Tyree?"

"Red lever, upper right of your panel, why?"

"Listen, Motherfucker," I say, my tone deadly serious when I see my face side-by-side with Gren's on the front screens, "we let you live. We should have killed you when we had the chance."

"Mighty bold talk, little Earth girl," his voice is derisive. "Pretty cocky coming from a defenseless breeder."

"Go to hell." I flip off the comm, my face flicks off the screen and I shout to Tyree, "Where are the controls to the laser cannons?" And where the heck is Axxios?

"You don't know how to shoot them, *Grace*. Computer, call Axxios to the bridge!" he orders again.

Our ship heaves as Gren fires another shot at us, closer this time, but still a miss. He laughs, obviously enjoying taunting us.

"I knew this would be too easy," he chides, "this isn't even sporting. Primitive animals flying a ship. Frankly, I was surprised a bunch of gladiators and breeders figured out how to take off from Numa. You must be speed reading the manual as we speak," he chuckles.

Axxios flies through the bridge doors, completely naked. Tyree vacates his chair as golden-skinned Axx slides into his spot in one smooth move.

Tyree switches to a different station and flips switches frantically. I hear the high whine of laser weapons gathering power. Go, Tyree!

I flick my comm back on, see my image jump to life in front of me and try to distract Gren while Axxios and Tyree prepare to fight or flee.

"You're right, we're out of our league," I admit. "You don't want to kill us. Let us live. There's a bounty on our heads, I've heard we're worth more alive than dead." Through the magic of technology, it feels like I'm looking straight into his evil, terrifying eyes, even though I know he can't really see me, just my image. You'd think this would chill me to my marrow, but all I can feel is seething rage.

Tyree fires a shot. It misses.

"Recalibrating," he shouts, his fingers moving on the panel in front of him with lightning speed.

I hear the lasers powering up and then he fires again—a direct hit into the belly of the cartel vessel just as Axxios steps on the gas. We move so fast I'm thrown against my seatback with enough force the flesh of my cheeks presses back against my bones.

"Take that!" I shout, even though Gren's repulsive face has flickered off the screen. My face is still up there. I see ten-foot-tall normally-demure Grace, her face squeezed in anger, arm raised in a fist. I look for all the world like an angry warrior. Rather than being embarrassed, it's thrilling to see that powerful woman on the screen.

Captain Zar crashes through the doors, "Can I help?"

"Enemy ship is dead in space back there," Axxios gloats still focused out the windows. Interesting how raising one's middle finger in anger seems to translate so well between different species a million miles away in space. "We're safe, but I'm not slowing until we're in the next sector."

The anxiety level on the bridge promptly reduces ten notches, although Tyree and the pilot are still frantically checking readouts on their computers. I glance over at Zar. The half-man, half-lion is completely nude and totally comfortable. I still forget, most of these gladiators fought naked in the arena for years. Clothing still seems optional to them.

"Can't hear any of their space chatter, Axxios. We've definitely put some distance between us. Nice maneuver. I'm glad you were here. I couldn't navigate fast enough," Tyree admits.

"For a male who's never fired a laser before, I'd say your direct hit to their hull more than made up for slow responses at the helm. We'll do some more drills tomorrow, Tyree. You're coming along well; you'll be more than proficient in time."

"MarZan cartel?" Zar asks.

"Not just MarZan, but our former captain, Gren," Tyree's voice drips with disgust. "Glad we overthrew the *motherdracker.*"

"That was a close call. It's getting harder to stay one step ahead of them. We're going to need a complete overhaul on Emirus. Axxios is right, we need to replace our broken hyperdrive. Glad we'll have the credits from Grace's performance. Thanks, Grace." Zar turns his head to look at me and smiles, his long, sharp canines flashing.

I hear chattering outside the bridge door and then it bursts open, with everyone on the ship spilling into this relatively small room. Most of the males are nude, the women are all wearing t-shirts of varying lengths. Everyone's talking at once, most asking variations of "WTF?"

Sometimes it still surprises me to look at my shipmates when we're gathered together. All the alien males are huge, muscular gladiators of different species. There's a spotted one, a silver one, and another who looks like a Neanderthal, as well as other aliens of various species. We've been together long enough now that we've become like a little family.

Tyree gives a quick rundown of the MarZan attack, giving most of the credit to Axxios and even praising my small part in it.

"Sounds like you *dracked* them up pretty good with the laser cannon," Dax praises. "Way to go, brother."

The corners of Tyree's mouth lift almost imperceptibly, and his shoulders pull up and back. He's proud—he should be.

"We'll touch down on Emirus in a few days," Zar continues. "The three days of performances will give us time to obtain new call letters and install important upgrades. Since MarZan knows our ship name, we'll need a new one."

"This time we'll take a vote," Anya, Zar's curly-haired human mate, interrupts. "Maddie, can you label a pot with the words 'new name' and put it in the dining hall? We'll gather all suggestions."

"Let's fill the pot with great ideas," Zar says. "Get some sleep."

People file out quickly. I haven't forgotten why I came to the bridge in the first place. I couldn't tolerate being alone in my room. After the attack, it's even clearer to me that I won't be able to duck out of my responsibilities. Although it's totally ridiculous, just thinking about these upcoming concerts ramps up my anxiety. I hope Tyree's generous offer to help me still stands.

Tyree

"Tyree," Axxios catches my attention. "I could never go to sleep after that close call. I'll drag in a mattress and sleep on the bridge until we leave Emirus. You can go to your cabin. I'm fine here."

I protest. I don't want to be derelict in my duty, but Axxios insists.

Grace is still at the comms panel, eyes following my every move, waiting patiently. I'm sure she wants to talk, that's why she wandered in here hours ago. I gently grasp her wrist and walk with her into the hallway.

I hear a lot of happy noise drifting toward us from the mess hall. I've discovered that almost dying makes people hungry—and aroused. My hunch is most of the other males will be eating a snack just long enough to check in with the female they were mated with when we were at the mercy of our captors. If the female is interested, there will be loud bedroom activity going on behind many closed doors in less than half an *hoara*.

My cabin is in a different direction than Grace's. I pause and she pulls me to the side of the hall and pierces me with her soft blue gaze.

"I came to the bridge to ask you to help calm me, Tyree. But wow. I certainly encountered a different side of myself tonight. I can't believe I looked him straight in the eye like a total badass," she laughs. "I'm still not sure I'll be able to sleep even though I know it's irrational. Do you think you could...use your powers to help me?" She glances away.

"Of course, that's why I offered. Grace, you just kicked ass on the bridge. You stood up to Gren, looked into his grotesque, vicious face and gave him hell. You wanted to fire lasers and destroy that ship. And yet the idea of playing your beautiful music sends you over the edge? I don't understand."

She looks at the floor, deep in thought. "It's a fear I've fought for a long time. It's not logical, I know." She shrugs.

"It's such a disconnect. On the bridge with Gren your hands were steady as a sniper's, now they're starting to tremble when you just think about the concert." My throat tightens in sympathy for her, she's struggling so hard. I tamp down the urge to hold those hands and kiss her palms.

"I never said my fears make sense, Tyree. That's why it's called a phobia. It's unreasonable. That doesn't make it any less real. Will you help me?"

Chapter Three

TYREE

"Let's go somewhere private," I gently grab her upper arm and head toward the solarium, my favorite room on the ship. The floor-to-ceiling windows that encircle eighty percent of the bullet-shaped room, as well as the see-through dome, provide a great view of the universe.

Grace edges to one of the panes and looks out quietly for a moment. "So vast. So beautiful," her voice is low and filled with awe.

"Yes," I admit earnestly, but I'm paying more attention to the lovely woman at my side than the expanse of dark space.

"Grace, have you ever wondered why you have this performance, what did you call it, phobia?"

She takes in a deep breath and slowly releases it through pursed lips like she's gaining control of her emotions. "No."

"Maybe if you give it some thought—"

"I haven't wondered, Tyree, because I already know."

There's a long silence. "Okay. You don't have to talk about it if you don't want to." My hand reaches out to stroke her arm, but I snatch it back before I make contact.

"It's not that. It's just...my response is totally out of proportion, you know?"

"I don't understand."

"The reasons don't seem that big a deal when I say them out loud. I think other people will think they sound small or petty, even ridiculous. This is about something that happened a lifetime ago. Other people would have moved on with their lives and followed their dreams. They wouldn't still be affected so profoundly by something a jerk did over a decade ago.

"And me? I serve people breakfast drinks instead of living the life I want because it distressed me so deeply. If I tell you the truth I'm afraid you'll judge me, think less of me...not like me."

Those last three words were spoken so low I barely heard them. "I'm not other people, Grace. Give me a chance." I want to divulge just how much I like her but now's not the time.

Slowly at first, she tells me about a male in a parental role she had as a child. She tells me a handful of abusive things he said and did to her. Somewhere in the middle of her story, she lets me hold her small hand in mine. Toward the end, she's cuddled next to me, her head on my chest, my arm around her shoulder.

I've had male hormones coursing through my body for weeks, but I think this is the first moment I've felt truly, fully male. I have my female in my arms. I'm providing her comfort.

"I don't think less of you. The real Grace is the one I saw an *houra* ago on the bridge. She was standing in her full power in front of a vicious bully with no thought of her own safety. This fear you have comes from the primitive part of your brain that doesn't listen to reason. There's nothing I'd like more right now than to help you with it, to calm you. When you're relaxed, I get more access to the real Grace." I swallow, then announce bravely, "I like her a lot."

She rewards me by looking deeply into my eyes. There's something about her gaze, this connection, that makes my heart squeeze in my chest.

"Tyree, when you...crawl into someone's mind, can you read their thoughts?"

She's afraid I'll violate her privacy. It's my job to reassure her. "It's...a challenge. I developed the skill of pushing thoughts and feelings *at* the other person, rather than taking thoughts and feelings *from* them." Then I tell her a strong, simply truth, "I'd never hurt you."

"Good. I wouldn't want you to read my mind. I'm too private for that."

She places her palm on my cheek, then sifts her fingers through my hair. I shut down every iota of awareness, every other particle of my thinking, and focus on this one thing—her gentle touch. *Drack* my cock at this moment. *Drack* its pulsing neediness. This non-sexual, gentle contact is more important than anything else.

I ease into her mind like a whisper of a breeze and press a calming gust of peaceful energy toward her. In less than a *minima* she takes the first relaxed breath I've seen her inhale since Zar told her about the concerts.

She moves her hands to my shoulders and begins to hum. It's a lilting melody that reminds me of folk tunes we used to sing on Larian. Her body sways with the music and I move with her. Other than standing on my father's feet and "dancing" with him when I was a youngling, I've never danced before.

The intimacy of moving with this female, <u>my</u> female, might be as close as I ever get to the fantasies that haunt me day and night. I breathe in her scent as I place my hands chastely at her waist. I tamp down the urge to lodge my fingers in her hair and press her mouth close for kisses. I discard the urgent thoughts of moving my hands lower and pressing her against my insistent cock. I focus only on the connection we're sharing right this moment.

She expels a soft sigh. I feel her muscles relax even more. Her face rests on my pectoral muscle, I can feel her gentle humming on my skin. The feel of her soft body pressed to mine, the beauty of her simple tune is like a precious gift. She's allowing me to see little glimpses of her soul. The more I get to know her, the more connected I feel.

Grace

I wake in my bed the next morning filled with a feeling of peace like nothing I've ever felt before. Growing up in total chaos with my mom stole any sense of safety I might have had as a child. My muscles feel loose, my thoughts are calm.

Then fear slams into my brain. I let my guard down with Tyree last night! I danced with him, for goodness sake. For weeks I've been trying to hide my attraction, but I'm certain falling into his arms and humming softly against his warm skin gave that away.

My hand flies to my throat in fear as my mind bombards me with worry thoughts. I was a virgin by choice when I came aboard this ship because I made a conscious decision as a child that I never wanted to be with a man. Hearing my mom panting and moaning in the next room under some nameless guy scared and disgusted me.

The men came and went, the type of drugs my mom was high on changed with availability, but the behaviors—her indiscriminate fucking, her neglect of her daughter—they stayed the same. Oh, and as I got older, the look in the men's eyes changed, too.

At a young age, I learned who people really are—weak, needy, demanding, easily addicted, and selfish. And straight or sober, men want to stick penises into vaginas. It seems to mean nothing more than a moment's pleasure. It's gross and meaningless and I made a promise to myself I wouldn't partake. I don't need it. I'm above it.

The time I spent with Shadow, the forced mating in that awful cell, the physical pain—that just cemented my decision to stay happily single, unattached, and non-sexual.

I have my music. It brings me peace and joy and will never leave me or call me names or bitchslap me. I can have a great life, even a million miles from Earth. All I need are my new friends, my own little room, and my instruments.

But for the first time in my life, I feel attraction to a male who's not up on a movie screen. I have to be honest with myself, last night in the solarium it wasn't just my throat that was humming. My entire body was humming with the awareness of Tyree's masculine presence.

It's like I'm riding a whirlwind. So many thoughts are flying through my brain at once. Even more interesting is what's going on in my body. Everything I've tamped down for the last twenty-six years has escaped from the container I've kept it in. With a vengeance!

My nipples pull into hard points just remembering those moments. Awareness awakens between my legs. I'm acutely conscious of one particular spot which is sending me increasingly urgent signals. It wants pressure. I build up my courage to explore and realize I'm damp. Energy is pooling in my stomach—maybe lower.

I use my timeworn formula to pull my mind away from these sexual thoughts and feelings. I think of a new combination of musical chords and rhythms. Not working!

I grab String Thing. Music helps. It's always helped. My fingers are clumsy and nothing I do makes my brain pay attention to anything other than the drumbeat of my pulse, the tingle of my nipples, and the wetness of my core.

In the past I read a lot on the Internet about sexuality, arousal, and attraction trying to figure out why I wasn't like any of the other girls at school: preoccupied with boys, flirtatious, and promiscuous. I never really found the answers I was looking for. And now this. Urgent sexual need is snaking along every nerve and synapse in my body.

How many times in the span of two months can a person's whole life change and come crashing down? First, I'm abducted from Earth and involved in a revolution. Now my whole sense of self is hijacked.

Nope. I'm having none of this. I'm returning to normal, at least my new normal. I'm going to take a shower and get dressed. I'm going to carry my instruments to the solarium, and I'm going to play. I'll dive into the enchanting altered state of my music. The place where hours can pass as though they're minutes. The state where Grace disappears and is so fully in the moment she has no thoughts but the present.

I'm going to avoid handsome Tyree of planet Larian. I'm going to figure out a way to be calm all day and go to sleep tonight under my own power. I don't need help from the gorgeous male I danced with last night. I am not interested in him. Whatever aberrant behavior is going on in my body right now is a response to fear and sleep deprivation. I'm still the Grace who is not attracted to anyone. I don't need males. I certainly don't need Tyree.

Tyree

I tried all day to think of anything but the moment Grace and I shared in the quiet of the solarium last night. I'll admit I've been unsuccessful. I've been humming the tune we danced to last night. My life was simpler before my *dracking* Transformation.

The constant erections. The obsession with Grace. I need to figure out how to manage myself, manage my body. I'm going to find Shadow—he's in a relationship now, he must have done something right with his female. At least he's been a male his whole life, which is a credential I don't share.

I shower, bind my loincloth so tightly it hurts, and search for him. Ever since he bonded to Petra and realized he had nothing to prove to anyone, he rarely goes to the *ludus*, the gymnasium, to work out. He could be anywhere on the ship as he experiments with new things: from navigating on the bridge, baking in the kitchen—which some of the males tease him about—to tinkering in the engine room.

I find him in the last place I look, the *ludus*. Interestingly, he's not lifting weights or sparring. He appears to be trying to ensure none of the other males on the ship are watching his female, Petra, who's working out on the rope they've hung from the ceiling. He's standing between the males and her, staring at them, arms crossed over his chest, and glowering.

"Shadow," Petra calls, "come twirl the rope for me." She gives him a sexy smile. He trots over, grabs the rope and forces it into lazy circles as she goes through a dizzying routine, most of it with her head facing the floor and her feet toward the ceiling. They're talking in low tones that make me wonder if it's private verbal foreplay. By the look on Shadow's face and the erection at his hips, I believe I'm right.

Even though he and I are friends, I still harbor resentment at the way he treated Grace when they were forced to mate. He was so angry then, so closed off to anyone and anything—especially his emotions. But he found Petra and mellowed. He smiles frequently now and wants to help everyone on board. Grace forgave him. I try to forgive him, too.

I don't want to interrupt them, so I grab a bar someone else was using, take about half the plates off, and lie back on the bench to press some weight. It's still heavy, but I don't need a spotter. I'll just keep an eye on Shadow and catch him when he's done flirting with his female.

After a few *minimas*, my arm muscles are quivering. I can't do this anymore. I saunter over, acting casual.

"Hey, Shadow, got some time?"

"Sure, Tyree. I'll catch you at dinner, Petra." He leans over and kisses her smack on the lips, then cups the globes of her ass and grins at her. "Later," he promises, his eyes molten with lust.

This proves one thing, people can change. He's not the angry, isolative male I met a few lunar cycles ago.

"What's up, brother?" he asks.

I'm honored. The gladiators use that term with each other. I never thought I would be on the receiving end of the word.

He pointedly takes one look at the sides of my loincloth, bound so tightly the fabric is cutting into my skin and turning it purple. "Female trouble?" He winks at me.

"Can we get out of here, Shadow?" Every male on the ship can't wait to get an earful of this conversation. As a child, I was taught that gossip was the province of old ladies, but I've never met a bunch of people more gossip-prone than a roomful of gladiators.

We walk for a while, then end up in the small, rectangular dining hall. The undecorated room is deserted except for Maddie who's puttering around in the adjoining kitchen making so much noise she could never overhear us.

"I'm interested in a female..." I realize what a fool I am, coming to Shadow of all people to speak about Grace. They were thrown into a cell together and forced to mate. He was an asshole to her at best, cruel at worst. She's forgiven him, quite publicly in fact. When they're thrown together on the ship they're cordial to each other. But talking about her might make both of us uncomfortable.

"You're interested in Grace. Everyone knows it. Not a se-cret." He shrugs.

Why exactly did I come to Shadow for advice? I forgot what a dick he could be.

"Yes," I nod my head, why argue when he knows the truth. "I want to get to know her. I want her to...like me. I have no idea what to do."

"And you came to me?" he laughs. "I was a complete *drack* to Petra when we met. It was a miracle she saw through my shitty side to the charming male underneath." He gives me a lopsided grin and a wink.

I rise from my seat. I could die of old age waiting for Shadow to say something helpful.

"Sit down, brother. I wasn't always a *dracking* gladiator, before that I was a *dracking* playboy. I have some moves."

"I don't want moves, Shadow. Grace is sweet. She's a ball of nerves. She's shy. Getting to know her shouldn't be a <u>move</u>. It should be like unwrapping a delicate package. It should be like stroking a fragile *amantine* wing."

"You did need me for something, Tyree. You needed to have this talk so you could say that. See? You know exactly what you need to do."

"What the *drack*? What are you talking about?"

"You just wrote your own playbook, Tyree. You described her perfectly. She *is* sweet and fragile. You need to pursue. Females love that. Sit with her at meals, talk to her, ask her to play her music for you. Let her talk. Tenderly unwrap the package, just like you said. You'll be fine."

I internally replay what he said, but it isn't as helpful as he thinks. Frankly, though, I don't believe he has much more to teach on this subject. Perhaps he could help with another pressing problem.

"The erections, Shadow? Seriously, they're constant."

"Still? I thought things would slow down a bit. Daily?"

"Daily? Are you kidding? Try five times a day. Worse when she's around, and I'm sure you heard I'm supposed to be helping her reduce her anxiety about this upcoming performance. Last night I calmed her and she stepped into my arms and danced with me."

"Good for you, my male. See? You don't need my help."

"It torched fire to the very blood in my veins all night long. And today." I glance down toward my cock. "I'm powerless."

"I read that if you perform multiplication tables—"

"Did that, got up to the seventeens. I must have read the same article on the Intergalactic Database. That was difficult mental gymnastics, but my erection could still dent metal."

I glance toward the kitchen, hear the water running and Maddie singing something that sounds wildly out of tune. I stand up, untie my loincloth, rearrange myself, and rewrap.

"Thanks, Shadow. I'll figure this out. You're a good friend."

"I do have one piece of advice, brother. You can't keep putting your cock in a tourniquet. You're going to cut off circulation."

Chapter Four

TYREE

Axxios and I spent several *hoaras* going over countless scenarios on the bridge. First, we replayed what happened last night with the cartel, down to the most minute detail. Then we brainstormed and practiced responses to other situations that might arise. I know I'm getting more proficient. No pressure—it's just a matter of life and death for everyone on board.

"Don't worry, Tyree, we'll keep practicing every day. You're actually a quick study," Axxios tells me. "I dragged my mattress in here yesterday. I'm not going anywhere until our mission to Emirus is complete. Go get some sleep."

"Thanks, Axxios. Think up some more scenarios we can run through tomorrow."

"Will do, my male."

I walk down the hall thinking about those words, "my male." That phrase did not describe me until twenty or so days ago when I came out of my coma after my Transformation. I still have trouble connecting those masculine words with myself. My Transformation has changed so much more than my body. It has changed how I think of myself.

I never gave gender much thought, since I didn't have any. Now that my body is male, and everyone sees me as male, I've had to step into that role in my own mind.

I have more questions than answers. What is masculine? What is feminine? Now that I have a penis, what really changes about me? How am I different? How am I the same?

My head spins with all these thoughts. Am I not the same person I was a lunar cycle ago?

"No." The answer resounds in my head. The addition of penis and balls and male hormones and *fiertos* of height has changed something fundamental about me. I feel different as I walk through my world. I want different things. I see my future differently.

Which leads my thoughts to Grace. We were friends a handful of days ago—chums. We had sleepovers full of laughter and watching vids for *drack's* sakes. I would still like sleepovers. But now I have no desire to lie there and watch vids.

In the lunchroom earlier I offered to come by her room tonight to give her a calming treatment. She averted her eyes and said she didn't think she'd need it. I knew she was lying, but let it go. She'll comm or come by if she needs me.

Just thinking about her makes my cock strain against my loincloth, putting in his opinion about what he'd like to do. By the feel of things, he's vigorously voting for her to come by later.

Shadow told me I should give my cock a name. That seemed ridiculous when we discussed it, but at this moment I think the name *Drackhead* would be appropriate. Don't worry *Drackhead*, I'll take a shower and you'll get your release.

On the walk back to my cabin, I realize I'm so agitated I won't be able to sleep for *hoaras*. I catch Shadow in the hallway.

"Got some time, Shadow? I wonder if you could give me another lesson on the Sillerian chainsticks. How about now?"

"Bad timing, brother. Petra and I have a date." His face slants into a lecherous grin. "In the *ludus*," he adds, eyebrows waggling as if this explains everything.

"Although I don't know what you're talking about, that's probably too much information."

"The rope, Tyree. The rope offers infinite possibilities." He's grinning so widely I think I can see his back molars.

I hold up my hand and turn toward my cabin. "More than enough information," I toss over my shoulder.

"I'll bring you a pair of chainsticks. You're good enough you can practice on your own," he calls after me.

I can't think of anything else I can do at this time of night, so I saunter to my room. I'll take a shower and try to get some sleep.

Grace

I got maybe an hour of restless sleep, and then bolted upright in a full sweat. I'd been dreaming about playing my instrument naked in front of a concert hall full of aliens. Thanks to Callista, who showed me vids of the opulent, humongous hall, I pictured every detail down to the crystal chandeliers and elegant blood-red curtains.

I'm panting, my mouth open, trying to catch my breath. Darn! I jump in the shower to cool down and wash the sweat off. Looking at the clock, I shake my head. It's only midnight. How am I going to get any rest tonight? If I don't work on my music and get my program ready tomorrow, I'm setting myself up for failure when I perform.

My worry about not sleeping ramps me up even more. If I don't intervene somehow, I'm guaranteed a sleepless night. Tyree could fix this—he's only steps away down the hall. I fight with myself for several minutes, not wanting to burden him, but even as I wage my internal battle, I know my feet are going to drag me to his door in desperation.

I knock and wait, considering turning on my heel and scurrying back to my cabin. I know Tyree and I used to be friends, but things seem so different lately.

"Thanks, Shadow. I'll practice with these for...*Drack*!"

Tyree opened the door stark naked, his arm up toweling his hair. He obviously thought I was Shadow.

His reflexes are quick; he's already slung his towel around his hips and is stammering his apologies. My eyes are wide in their sockets, I'm barely breathing, and I don't know whether my mind is trying hard to unsee what I just saw, or recreate the image as a permanent memory in my mind.

The Statue of David comes to mind. Only David ranks a paltry second place. My mind is currently cataloging every rigid muscle, every flat plane, the jut of his hip bone, the curve of his ass. Desire fires along every synapse in my body. My nipples harden, feeling as if they've been tweaked.

His body is perfection. And oh my God, he's observing my complete hormonal overload right this minute. I haven't heard a word he's said. I can't focus on the information penetrating my ears, because the entire capacity of my mind is fixated on what I just saw.

"Grace. I'm going to close the door," his voice pierces my mental fog. "You're going to knock. I'm going to open it and then we'll pretend the last few moments never happened. Okay?" He shuts the door.

Instead of raising my hand to knock, I glance down the hall toward my room and wonder if I can scurry there and slam the door behind me before he realizes I've run away. I decide I'm never going to knock. I'm never going to see him again. I'll hide in my room and not come out, even to eat, until one of us dies of old age. Or starvation.

"Come in, Grace." He must have realized I'm not going to knock, so he's opened the door, the towel chastely tucked around his waist.

When I'm unable to order my feet forward, he gently grasps my upper arm and maneuvers me past his threshold.

"Sorry. I thought you were Shadow, he was going to bring me some chainsticks."

"No problem," I hear myself say. "Totally understandable." I do understand, actually. Nudity is such a big nothingburger on this ship. The males have no modesty whatsoever.

I realize we're both sitting on the edge of his bed. Not sure how that happened. I curb the urge to jump to my feet.

"Can't sleep," I confess.

"I figured. What happened?"

"Terrible dream. Playing naked in front of thousands of people. Woke up in a cold sweat."

He swallows hard. "If you'd like, I'll get dressed, calm you down, and lie on the floor near your bed. You'll be safe and I can give you another treatment in the middle of the night if you need it."

"No way, Tyree. I'd be a terrible person if I let you sleep on the floor. I won't hear of it. But I think you're right about staying with me tonight. How about I lay waaay over here on this side of the bed, and you lay waaay over on that side of the bed. Will that work?"

It's only now that I listen to my invitation that I realize how hard this will be. As if things weren't awkward with Tyree before this. As if my lifetime of avoiding attraction to men wasn't already beginning to crumble. His "big reveal" certainly isn't going to make me more comfortable.

I've still got the image of this nude Larian Adonis burned into my retinas, and now I'm going to be sleeping in the same bed with him.

And by his tilted head and compressed lips, I'm not sure this will be any easier on him.

"Sure. My bed or yours?"

How can he ask that? Is this male made of steel? Does he hear what he's asking? I want to crawl out of my skin, and he's completely unaffected. Whoops, not so unaffected. Mr. Happy has pitched a tent under his towel. Does this make me feel better or worse? I swallow, my mouth suddenly dry.

"Um, we're already here..." I shrug. Probably best to keep him out of my room. At some point, I'm going to be sleeping alone in there and I don't need to be haunted by ten thousand mind pictures of him in the very bed I have to sleep in.

"You can lie down if you'd like. I'll...get dressed and be right back," he says.

I step out of my flip-flops and slip under the covers, still wearing leggings and a t-shirt. He's taking a while in the bathroom. I hear him turn on the shower. Didn't he just get out of the shower? A thought arrows into my brain. Is he masturbating in there?

I'm imagining him in his shower, a mirror image of my own. Since his little strip show, I can now accurately picture every freaking inch of his skin, from scalp to toes. My mind abuses me with a portrait of him—his hip leaned against the metal wall, his head hung at an angle, his forearm muscles bunching as his long, strong fingers stroke his shaft. Then I picture him fisting himself and getting down to business, every muscle coiled as he readies himself to finish. I see in minute detail how his head lifts and tilts toward the ceiling, his knees bow slightly, and his release jets into the water circling the drain.

I clamp my jaw shut, trying to get a hold on my sexual urges, which are swamping me right now. My clit is throbbing. I'm now rerunning the movie I just produced in my head. I'm sure I've soaked my panties. The movie rewinds and now I'm in the shower with him—the water sluicing over us both. His fingers are plucking my nipples, sliding down my sides, then slipping between my folds.

Dear Lord, he is so sexy, and we're going to be bedding down for the night—together—in a few minutes. Then what? I realize my hands are itching to touch his bronze skin. Who am I fooling? I can't get the image of his penis out of my mind. I know exactly which specific inches of his skin my fingers long to touch.

"Stop it, Grace!" I whisper to myself, just as he opens the bathroom door. He's already turned the light off in there. He hustles to the other side of the bed and dives in wearing his blue jumpsuit.

"Computer, dim lights," he says.

We both sigh.

"This is awkward," he admits.

"Agreed. Maybe if we talk for a while it will take our minds off what just happened. What are your favorite foods?" I ask randomly.

"Anything but nutrition bars."

"Good answer. I only ate them for a week when we were in the cellblock and I'd be happy to never see one again. Your turn to ask."

"What do you miss most about Earth?"

I have to think. The obvious things, the ones every other girl on the ship would mention aren't on my list. Parents? No. Siblings? Got none. Pets? Nope. Job? That would be a big no. What do I miss? I realize I was just waiting for something to happen in my life.

"I didn't mean to stump you, Grace. I thought that would be an easy thing to answer."

"It was a sobering thought, Tyree. There's a term in music called vamping. It means a few meaningless chords that you just keep playing over and over while you wait for something to happen. Like when you're waiting for an actor to come on stage and they're late. It's boring, just a time filler. Your question made me realize that's what my life was. I was just vamping, waiting for something better to come along."

"And now? Are you still vamping?"

"You sure ask hard questions, Tyree. As hard as the last two months have been—and as hard as the next few days are going to be—no. I think I've quit vamping, Tyree. I think I'm starting to have a real life."

He gives me one of his thousand-megawatt smiles, and he never looks away. "I'd like to be part of your real life, Grace. I'd be honored if you'd count me as a friend."

"I do, Tyree. And I'd like to get to know you better."

He turns up the wattage on his smile, then, "Okay, it's getting late. Lie on your side facing me."

I'm quick to comply. If only I could fall into a deep sleep and wake up rested.

He reaches up and nestles his hand on the back of my neck. His touch is so gentle and warm it feels more intimate than a kiss. We're so close, even though the lights are dim, I'm certain he can read every thought that crosses my face.

"Computer, lights out," I command through parched lips.

Time slows down in the complete darkness. I can hear his breathing. His soft puffs of breath whisper across my face. My eyes are closed, my mouth slightly open. I slip my tongue to moisten my lips and the image of putting my tongue on his cock jumps into my mind.

My muscles tighten at just the word "cock" in my mind. That is not a word I use, not in speech with others, not even in my own thoughts. But there it is. What do you know? Sweet, modest Grace has an entire vocabulary of smutty words and images and desires that have been cued up, waiting to be unleashed.

And speaking of unleashed...wait. I experience that feeling of his mind reaching out to mine. As if he's asking permission before crossing the threshold. I open my awareness to him and a gust of calming energy drifts in. He deposits the tranquility and leaves, like a puff of smoke moving in a stiff wind.

My muscles relax. My thoughts get fuzzy. I could fall asleep so easily if I just allow it.

Chapter Five

GRACE

I wake to the sound of Tyree in the shower. You've got to give that male credit—he's clean. My spidey senses tell me he doesn't have OCD, he's just taking care of his morning hard-on.

"No, Grace," I order myself. "You will not watch an instant replay of the movie you produced last night! No more fantasies of him fisting himself in the shower." I propel myself out of bed as if I've been ejected, and scurry toward my room.

After showering, I pull my clothes on in record time, grab my instruments and hurry to the solarium. Other than Tyree, this place is the only thing that calms me. I love the view. It's dark, except for a myriad of stars. Like black velvet strewn with thousands of diamonds. Off to the right, there's a purple nebula, maybe millions of miles away, with the most beautiful spectrum of colors.

I perch on one of the chairs positioned at the back window and just soak up the unspeakable beauty and peace. The concert doesn't exist. The gorgeous Larian doesn't even exist. Just me. And my mind settles into calm, quiet peace.

I begin to play the song Callista informs me is the one that's being listened to the most frequently over the Intergalactic Database. It's my favorite, too. It starts slow, then builds to a crescendo, and ends abruptly. It's both romantic and dramatic.

My hands are barely idle for a moment before they begin a new tune. These notes are melancholy, slow, lugubrious. The emotion they evoke is longing, yearning.

I feel like I have two personalities. Part of me is producing this exquisitely somber piece that depicts desire—unfulfilled desire. And another part of me is watching my internal reel of Tyree favorites, all the greatest hits of the handsome male from planet Larian.

Tyree smiling and joking in the dining hall. Tyree chumming around with Shadow as they tease relentlessly in their amusing brother-from-another-mother style. But mostly, my visuals are stuck on an endless loop of him in the shower, leaning his hip against the metal wall, his masculine hand clutched around his hard cock. It's so specific, down to the water dripping off the tip of his ear, that you'd think I watched it in person, rather than in my mind's eye.

My core clenches, moistening. Yeah, yearning. My fingers are simply acting out the desire I'm feeling in other parts of my body.

Tyree

I barely cross the threshold of the dining hall before I realize Grace isn't there. She's probably still practicing her music in the solarium. She must be so engrossed in playing that the passage of time escaped her. I go to collect her.

The door to the solarium opens so quietly she doesn't know I've breached her private space. I take this moment to fully observe this female. Her chair is canted at an angle toward the back windows, so I only see her profile. Dear Gods, she is exquisite. I hate to tear my eyes from her nimble fingers as they dance across the keys and buttons of the instrument in her lap. But I want to look at her mercurial expressions.

She frowns, her brows knitted together, when her fingers evoke sadness. Her shoulders straighten and her chin tilts upward when the music becomes joyful and lively. My chest clenches beneath my ribs when I watch her. I want to connect with those emotions.

She'll expose those feelings to her instruments, alone here in this room, but she has never exposed herself like that to me. She's allowed me to see her panic—that was too hard for her to hide. But these tender emotions, the fervor, the longing, those are always kept tightly shuttered behind her calm facade.

I yearn to see those emotions parade across her face. I want to share things with her. I want to talk long into the night. I want to make her laugh. I want to hear her moan in ecstasy.

Oh, *Drackhead* likes this thought. He pulses in approval. Yes, *Drackhead*, that too. But I want so much more. I want to touch more than her body. I want to touch her soul.

She's my truemate. To be honest, I've known it for weeks, maybe longer. Maybe since the first signs of my Transformation. But I've pushed away the awareness. At first, I was in disbelief that I could transform without another Larian present. But obviously that's not true.

I transformed to be with Grace.

Frankly, it doesn't matter if she's my truemate. What does that mean, anyway? That by some freak twist of biology my DNA bonded with her DNA? I don't want a truemate because of some chemical formulation. I want a mate who I can connect with. Whose *soul* I connect with. And that is Grace, this woman I'm watching with wonder right now.

I can see her soul, her passion, written across her face. I want that passion directed at me. I have to figure out how to be on the receiving end of that.

I've started already. She trusts me. At least she trusts me to help her, to calm her. If Shadow was here he'd point out that I'm already sharing her bed—that's a start.

"Grace," I call gently. I hate to pull her out of the magical space she inhabits when she's composing. "Grace," I repeat louder. She startles, her fingers immediately stilling on her instrument.

"Oh!" Her mouth remains in that started 'O' shape, her eyebrows lifted. For a moment she looks afraid, as if she's in trouble.

"Dinnertime. I didn't want you to miss it."

"Dinner? I guess lunch is long over, huh?" Her face is placid now as if she's forced her fears away, deep inside so I can't see them. I wonder how often she does that—push all the delicate emotions she feels down under a facade of calm.

"Yes. Let me take you to dinner. Get a lot done today?"

She nods and gives me a bright smile. I've seldom seen her like this—almost happy and carefree. "My muse was on fire today. I couldn't stop creating new tunes. It was glorious! Today everything just flowed; it was like the music downloaded into my brain from somewhere else."

She really looks at me for the first time today. Then I actually see her face change, as if in slow motion. She pulls her lips from an upturned smile into a flat line. The shine dulls in her eyes. It's as if the real Grace made a brief appearance, and then she was banished, leaving the shell of Grace to carry on.

I want the real Grace. I realize I'll need to lay a foundation of trust, and then excavate to find the genuine Grace who hides underground and only sticks her head out from time to time.

"Let's go. Tonight's the vote to rename the ship. Did you suggest an idea?" I don't want to admit I almost submitted the name "Gift of Grace." Instead, I change the subject, "The mystery meat smelled particularly good." I smile at her. She returns a fake one. I'm beginning to see that the Grace I've known until today is only a pale replica of the one sheltering deep inside.

Grace

"Thanks for coming," Anya, Zar's mate, begins, her lips pulled into a happy grin. She looks excited and energetic as usual, with her sparkling green eyes and halo of brown curls.

She grabs the big, well-used pot off the banquet table where it's been sitting for the last few days and shakes it. "We've got lots of suggestions to change the name from the *Sweet Deliverance* since our cover's been blown by the bad guys. Let's remember, we're brainstorming."

The males all flinch in unison. That word must have translated badly. I picture a storm in a brain and the resulting image *is* pretty distressing.

"That means there's no such thing as a bad suggestion. No one is allowed to say anything derogatory about anyone else's idea. We're too nice for that, right?"

"Too nice unless it's Stryker's suggestion, then anyone is allowed to boo," Dax yells from the back of the room. Dax is the tallest male on the ship and resembles a Neanderthal with his sloping forehead. He's made a huge change since the insurrection, from scowling and angry to full of laughter and jests.

Stryker's scarred face is grinning from ear to ear at Dax's good-natured jibe.

"Yes, I agree," Anya nods her head, laughing. "We're all allowed to make fun of Stryker." He makes a mock scowl, then nods and affectionately claps Dax on his broad back.

"Okay," Anya calls loudly. "What I thought I'd do is read all the suggestions once. Callista, if you'd be so kind as to write them on the translation board and project it on the front wall. Then we can vote and keep narrowing things down until we get a clear consensus."

Callista steps forward, translator in hand. It looks like a basic computer pad the size of a piece of legal paper. I have no idea how the translation board works, but it allows us all to read in our native languages.

"Oh," Anya says distractedly as she pulls little slips of paper out of the pot and smoothes them into a pile. "It looks like I neglected to mention everyone should write their names on their suggestions. Well, actually, that's a good thing. We don't want this to be a popularity contest."

"I'll just read them without comment. Here we go. Sweet Freedom, Flying Freedom, Taste of Freedom, Free and Easy, Liberation. We've definitely got a theme going here. Just a few more." She flattens the last slips.

"Lovely Dahlia. I know I said I wouldn't comment, but Dax I never knew you were such a romantic. Awww."

Everyone looks toward Dax and Dahlia. She's flushed pink with embarrassment, but her eyes are shining sweetly as she looks directly at her male. It's so cute.

"We've got some good ones here. Now the last one, Battle-Scarred Warrior."

"Did you put that one in, Stryker?" Dax asks. "Want to name this vessel after your pretty face?"

This draws laughs from everyone, even Stryker who likes being included in the fun.

"Well, we've got lots to choose from. Let's vote, perhaps that will help us narrow it down."

A show of hands easily narrows it down to two: Liberation and Battle-Scarred Warrior.

"These two were pretty close in votes," Anya announces. "How about if the people who submitted these names give a little pitch about their idea? It says Doctore suggested Liberation. Anything to say?"

Doctore stands and strides to the front of the room. His skin is burnished mahogany. On Earth, I'd say his skin was scarified on a shoulder, pectoral, and most of his back. But I think this isn't elective, but rather, part of his species.

He was the teacher in the *ludus* before the insurrection. I understand he was a slave most of his life.

"This ship has been our liberation, our freedom, our salvation. It is the means to escape our pasts and build new futures." He sits down.

"So nicely put. Thanks, Doctore. And Battle-Scarred Warrior? There's no name on this." She holds up the scrap of paper.

We all look around, waiting for someone to take credit. No one volunteers. Anya asks a few of the men, especially the heavily-scarred ones like Shadow, Stryker, and Dax. Each in turn denies it.

"Okay, someone's shy I guess. Everyone's here. I'll take roll." As she goes through the list alphabetically, everyone denies ownership of the name.

"Zar? Is this yours?" He shakes his maned head.

There's only one member of the crew left. With each passing moment and each successive pair of eyes that land on her, Zoey's face becomes a darker shade of pink.

"Zoey?" Anya asks, her tone incredulous.

Zoey is by far the shyest person on the ship. In fact, she's the shyest person I've ever met. With less than twenty-five souls on this vessel, all in such close quarters, we know each other fairly well. Except for Zoey who rarely talks and prefers to hide in the shelter of Steele's burly, protective, silver arm.

"Busted," Maddie, the cook, calls as she gives Zoey a friendly look.

The shy female with limp, brown, shoulder-length hair stands and meekly walks to the front of the room.

"Just a few words, Zoey," Anya wheedles. "Why that name?"

She takes a deep breath and then her words come out in a soft rush. We all lean forward to hear her.

"Every male and female on this ship is a battle-scarred warrior. Some show it on their flesh, like Shadow and Dax. But we all carry it, don't we? Haven't we all been through many battles? And as sure as we're standing here we know we have many more to come.

"*Sweet Deliverance* was the best name for newly-freed slaves, but we've moved on. I want whoever we tangle with from now on to know every single one of us is a hardened warrior. We won't give up without a fight. I want the message to tell the cartel and whoever comes after us Don't. Fuck. With. Us." Although her voice started almost too soft to hear, her last four words come out loud and proud.

She looks completely different than I've ever seen her: spine straight, eyes bright, muscles tight. Now she morphs back to quiet Zoey as she slinks to her seat. I'd like to see more of the first Zoey. I vow to spend more time with her after I return from Emirus.

"Whoa," Anya comments in admiration. "Great speech. Shall we vote?"

It takes less than a minute to decide we'll be called Battle-Scarred Warrior. Even Doctore voted for that name. I don't think it's my imagination when I notice Zoey's chin lift a little higher and her shoulders thrust back a little farther as we celebrate the new name with glasses of what passes for champagne on board the *Battle-Scarred Warrior*.

Tyree was right, the mystery meat smelled fantastic tonight. The taste, however, was almost rancid. Maddie was a chef in her previous life on Earth. Someone told me she was a sous-chef at Spago, no small feat. If she couldn't make this meat taste good, no one could.

The males liked it, of course. Most of them have been slaves for so long, eating nutrition bars that tasted like sawdust and glue, they're happy to ingest anything that's been cooked and can be chewed. Every night, toward the end of the meal, one of them will yell out, "Hooray for the cook," to a resounding round of applause.

I eat the mystery veggie and mystery starch, but I'm unable to stomach the mystery meat. Maddie tells us what we're eating every night. She concocts these great names—sometimes sophisticated, sometimes fun. Tonight, she said we're eating *sacru sheswah* with *prendo* sauce, *marquet* florentine, and escalloped *vren*. Yeah, most of it tasted like shit, but it felt very upscale.

"Don't like the *sacru sheswah?*" Tyree inquires, cocking his head and eyeing my plate.

I stab my slab of meat with my fork and hold it up toward him. "Feel free," I offer. He motions for me to dump it on his plate.

"I think this is the best thing Maddie's made yet." He digs in, then with his mouth full yells, "Hooray for the cook!" The males chime in as usual. The women's plates all contain the remains of their uneaten meat. I roll my eyes at his praise for the awful dish.

"What?" he asks around a mouthful of food.

"It just didn't agree with me."

He finishes chewing and swallows. "Say it, Grace. Say you hated it. Go ahead."

"It wasn't that bad."

"Say it. Say what you feel. You didn't like it, did you?"

"No." I shiver thinking about the horrible taste and mouthfeel.

"You hated it. Say it."

I shake my head. What is he doing? He looks so serious. Why does he care? I gave him my leftovers.

"Whatever your circumstances were back on Earth, you're not there anymore. You're among friends. You can have your own opinions. You can say what you like and what you don't like and you can say you hated your *sacru sheswah*. Say it."

His eyes are so sober—intense. I know he means me no harm, so why am I holding my breath in fear?

He sees my worry and places his hand low on my thigh. He gently puts his thumb and forefinger on each side of my knee and pushes calm at me—and something else. Is he sending me an apology? I look into his brilliant green eyes and see it. Yes, a sincerely contrite look.

"Sorry, I got passionate there. I just thought, 'Grace should be able to say she didn't like her dinner.' Shouldn't you, Grace? Shouldn't you be able to say that?"

My mouth gets dry. Shit, why *was* that so hard? Why did I resist saying I didn't like it? Why couldn't I reveal I hated that crappy mystery meat?

His hand is still on my knee. He's still calming me. I can think clearly instead of my mind seizing up like a car engine that hasn't been oiled. A memory cascades back from almost twenty years ago.

One of my mom's "boyfriends" was having dinner with us. I can still picture every detail of that evening. Mom was high, her eyes glassy. She was pushing her food around on her plate. They'd argued earlier in the evening. Things were already tense. The guy, what was his name, Butch? Rowdy? Barbarian, that's right. It was during her biker phase.

Barbarian noticed I wasn't eating my peas and ordered me to finish what was on my plate. I was maybe in first grade, just this tiny little girl, and he was...well, he was a huge biker Barbarian. I was scared shitless and not about to argue. I stabbed the peas, one by one, trying to force them down my gullet, but evidently, that process wasn't fast enough.

"Eat them!" he screamed.

I glanced at Mom, I don't know why. By then I was certainly old enough to know that no one was coming to help me—definitely not her.

"Eat them!"

I gripped my spoon and shoveled a bunch of peas into my mouth, but he was so furious he grabbed the utensil from my hand and forced it past my teeth and into the back of my mouth. I remember it all: the gagging, the metallic taste of the spoon, the inability to both swallow and grab air. For a moment I thought I was going to die.

My tongue slides over the biting surface of my top front teeth. I can feel the rough scrape where he made a tiny chip in my brand new permanent tooth.

I remember having to run to the bathroom to throw up after that. I can picture the viscous green lump of peas in the toilet. I can smell it. I don't want to, but for a moment I relive the feeling of abject isolation I felt. I had no one. No one to help me. No one to run to. Just little Grace and her jagged front tooth.

I look around the dining hall. I haven't been "gone" long. No one noticed I was lost in the memory—no one but Tyree. He knows. He amps up the "wattage" of his treatment. My cheeks are heated, my jaw tight.

He moves his hand from my knee to the nape of my neck and pushes more serenity at me. It flows through me like a gently-moving brook. My nerves relax.

"I'll scrape our plates and get you back to your room, Grace. Give me a moment."

Chapter Six

TYREE

I offered to carry her back to her room, but she shook her head no. We quickly made our way through the hallways and I helped her over the threshold of her cabin. I sit in the chair after I settle her on the bed.

"I don't know what happened, Grace, but I know it was my fault. I'm sorry. I just wanted to help you see that you could be yourself here. You could say what you like and what you don't. I realize I made a mistake."

After a long pause, "Not really, Tyree. You didn't make a mistake. I was taught at an early age not to say no. Not to ask for what I want. I need to realize I'm a different person now. I have other options."

She kicks off her shoes and slides under the covers. "I tried to say no the other day. I didn't think it would be well received."

Zar. The concert. It couldn't have been more clear that she didn't want to do it.

"We pressured you, Grace. That wasn't right."

"Actually, it was. I know I should be stronger. Six hours of my anxiety is a small price to protect the lives of everyone on board. I understand. I want to perform those concerts on Emirus with every bone in my body. And my mind, it's on board, too. It's just my stupid emotions, they're stuck in the past."

"Okay, but I still shouldn't have pushed you like that in the dining room."

"The *sacru sheswah* tasted like shit. It shouldn't have taken an act of God for me to admit it." She gives me a shy smile. I'm glad to see it.

I have no idea what to do now. We have several hours before bed. I'm so new at this. "Do you want me to stay with you tonight? Or take off?

"You've been so kind, Tyree. I know I'll never get any sleep tonight without you. Would you mind sleeping with me tonight? I found a show about ice fishing on planet Tenre-hu. Fascinating. The fish they catch have twelve-inch-long teeth. Want to binge-watch?"

"Binge-watch?"

"Watch back to back until we fall asleep."

"The way you describe the program that will take about ten *minimas*."

"Oh, we can find something else..."

"Sure," I tell her.

Grace

Interestingly, after today's work in the solarium, I know I'll be fine for the technical part of my performance. I've already written down the program I want to play and put it in order. I think it will flow nicely from easy-breezy, to serious, to a big dramatic finish. If I was a robot, I'd be fine right now. But I'm a human, a very anxious human with a performance phobia, and my nerves are still on overdrive. Thank goodness for Tyree.

I glance over at him, grabbing my computer pad off the desk. He'd fit in great on Earth. A little plastic surgery on those sexy ears and he'd take Hollywood by storm. My stomach does a little flip as I look at him.

"You ready for me?" he asks. "If not, I'll just sit here and read."

"My program's complete. I'll just do some practicing tomorrow and I'll be all set." I try to look composed and upbeat as I attempt to calm my rising hormones.

Tyree moves the computer pad to the bed, then toes off his shoes and slides under the covers. Luckily, he's wearing a blue jumpsuit and not a loincloth like the other males wear most of the time. Some part of my brain believes this will provide an extra barrier between my lust and the object of my fantasies.

We get comfortable and start searching through the channels. The Intergalactic Database is supposed to carry the best vids of the known galaxy. All I know is I'd kill for some *Dexter* reruns.

After the better part of an hour, we settle on a wildlife program with National Geographic production values. The animals are amazing. It's fascinating, but I'm more interested in Tyree, whose big body commands my full attention.

For some reason, I'm not focusing on the upcoming performance—my nerves seem steady. I'm busy watching Tyree from the corner of my eye. He seems interested in the snow bear of planet Zath. I'm more engrossed in him.

I've never touched his ears. They're about five inches long and point up and back. They're alluringly sexy and look velvety soft.

"Can I feel your ear?" Did that actually pop out of my mouth? What possessed me to say that? What happened to my filter?

His head pivots my way, his eyes wide.

I hide my head in my hands and mutter under my breath, "Sooo politically incorrect."

"Well, I believe not that long ago I was encouraging you to ask for what you want. Go ahead."

"Really? That wasn't over the top?"

"Over the top? Yes. But go ahead."

The vid is forgotten as I turn, bending my knee and putting weight on my hip, so I can see him better. I reach up to touch the top edge, where ear meets head, then slide my fingers up the silky-soft skin to the tip of his ear. It doesn't end in a sharp point but isn't particularly rounded. My fingers explore behind, to the delicate skin that faces his head, then along the fascinating ridges inside the ear.

I take the time to study his face. His eyes are shuttered, his lips are slightly parted. His breathing is uneven, and his nostrils are flared. I've aroused him. I snatch my hand back as if it were on fire.

He startles back to the present, opens his mouth as if to say something, then snaps it shut again.

"Sorry," I say. "I shouldn't have done that."

"Why?"

"Uh. It was forward. It was..." a lover's touch.

He spears me with his glowing emerald gaze. I see an internal fight rage inside him and then, "My life has turned upside down, Grace. A slave for a quarter century—now free. Tiny and sexless—now tall and male. You'd think I'd need time to resolve things, to figure out who I am and what I want. But right now I know one thing with more certainty than anything I've ever known.

"I'm drawn to you, Grace. I want...I want to know you, to care for you, to protect you. The way you just touched me, Grace, I want that. And I want to touch you that way, too." His voice is husky and full of passion.

He's staring at me. I'm always beating around the bush, and here he is, holding nothing back. I feel like it's that moment in the *Wizard of Oz* when everything goes from black and white to color. Nothing can ever be the same as it was a moment ago.

Every nerve and synapse in my body comes online. I'm fully alive in a way I've never been before. He told me to ask for what I want. I'm usually so focused on taking care of everyone around me I'm seldom aware of my own needs. I shut off those pesky things like wishes and desires years ago. And now they're hurtling at me, like meteors bombarding a defenseless planet, crashing all around me.

What do I want? More.

"Yes." I hope it's all I have to say. It is. Because he reaches out in slow motion. His eyes pinning mine, making certain this is what I want. "Yes," I repeat, to leave no doubt.

The smallest smile crosses his face, then his muscles tighten, he looks so serious, as his long, strong fingers land softly on my chin, then travel up my jawline to my ear. He traces the inner circles of my ear, causing me to shiver.

He lifts a questioning eyebrow, perhaps wondering if it was a good shiver or a bad one. I tilt my head toward him and press his hand closer. His fingers sift through my hair and land firmly on the back of my head. Leaning in, he pulls me gently toward him. We meet in the middle, our lips colliding sweetly.

I can barely breathe, my thoughts are spinning.

The press of his mouth is soft lips with a firm touch. He slides his lips back and forth against mine. This intimacy, just this, catapults me into a different place, a different self. It's a rite of passage. I know my life will never, ever be the same from this moment forward. The gentle, almost restrained touch of his flesh on mine places me solidly into uncharted territory.

This isn't friendship anymore. This is sexual. I've crossed the line and am now a sexual being.

I'm tired of thinking and worrying and second-guessing. This feels too fantastic. More. I want more.

I reach up and crook my arm around his neck, effectively linking us together. "Mmmm," I say, and shiver again, the vibration tickling and arousing at the same time.

He leans back slightly, then bestows on me another kiss. Soft and brief and chaste. It ignites a fire in me. The heat flies along my synapses from lips to nipples to clit. Arousal.

I want more kisses.

And he complies—harder, just the slightest bit more pressure. Many kisses. Raining kisses. Full-on kisses. Side-of-the-mouth kisses. Now cheek and eyelid and nose kisses. And back to my lips where he nibbles their fullness. Almost as if he wants to pluck them with his own.

My breath is coming in little pants. My body is alive in ways I've never felt before. Some hidden, prehistoric instinct arrows a picture into my brain—me straddling his lap, riding him. Slow down, Grace. Allow this kiss to blossom.

Both my hands surround him now, hidden in his soft hair, pressing his mouth closer to mine. My hands roam down his back, touching material-clad shoulder blades, strong muscles, and the narrow inlet of his waist.

"Mmmm," an inarticulate moan escapes me. Perhaps it's this noise that spurs him to explore further. The tip of his tongue slips out and slides along the seam of my lips. I'm sure he feels my smile, the corners of my mouth curve up. He presses harder, and my sluggish brain finally comprehends his attempt to enter.

My tongue sneaks out to greet him. The tips of our tongues dance shyly for a moment, and then more confidently. I feel playful and deadly serious at the same time. I've talked and eaten with this tongue for twenty-six years, how is it

I've never experienced this feeling? This warm, yearning, sensuality? My core is tight and hungry, with just these little kisses.

Then he deepens the kiss, pressing into me, breaching the threshold. There is a lovely yielding sensation. An exchange of power. The passing of the baton. He's in charge.

And now I'm playing with him. Circling his tongue with mine. It's a game of give and take. No winners, no losers. Just this exciting, sensual dance. He brushes my tongue with his. A burst of electrical energy floods my pelvis. I want pressure, stroking...penetration? So compelling. So this is how people get carried away. The urge feels so strong, and yet I know I'm completely in control of myself.

Tyree pulls away, causing me to drag my lids open to look at him. "So good," he breathes, almost no sound to his words. "Takes my breath away." He's panting, his face more serious than I've ever seen it.

He jumps off the bed, turns his back, unzips his jumpsuit and fumbles under his clothes. I assume he's rearranging himself. If I could, I'd be doing the same. It's just that my desires aren't so obvious—the painful yearning is internal.

"Best kiss I've ever had," I laugh. "You too?"

"Absolutely," he tosses me a molten look over his shoulder. "Incomparable."

"This is one for the books. Thirty-five and twenty-six and we've never been kissed. It would be an oddity on Earth," I tell him.

"I can't imagine sharing that with anyone but you, Grace. That," he glances at my lips and I see his muscles tighten with desire, "was worth waiting for."

"I agree." I take mental inventory of my thoughts and emotions and the interesting whirling energy slicing through my body. For the first time in days, I'm calm without Tyree's psychic treatments. My body's on fire, but I feel great. "No regrets," I reassure both myself and him.

"I don't know if I can do any more of that without...losing control and pushing you, Grace. Can we take a break?"

I nod. He's right. Neither of us has enough experience to step on the breaks if things get even more incendiary.

"Hungry? I know this place that serves a great *sacru sheswah*," he grins and winks.

"How did you know that's what I was craving?" Practically jumping out of bed, I glance in the mirror and notice my too-bright eyes and just-kissed lips. I think of the other females' reactions if they knew what went on in this bed. I decide I don't give a flying fuck what anyone might think. All I know is Tyree was right, if we don't get out of this room right now things are going to progress way too fast.

Tyree

We're like two kids who've run away from home and don't know where they're going, just going "away." I try not to let her see my delighted shock when she playfully grabs my hand and pulls me toward the dining area.

I never spent much time in a kitchen, but she seems competent enough as she stands in front of the open door of the food cooler and rummages around in there.

"You really liked the sack of shit, right?"

I don't believe I've ever heard her cuss before—well, except for what she said to Gren—she was spectacular when she did that. I've also never seen her so relaxed. I decide I definitely like this new Grace.

"Sack of shit, Grace? Did that translate correctly?"

"*Sacru sheswah*, sack of shit...whatever." She shrugs.

"*Sacru sheswah*? Yes, loved it. It was so delicious. Is there any left?"

"By the look on the Earth women's faces, there's bound to be a ton of it in here somewhere. Here it is."

She lifts a container between thumb and forefinger as if she can barely tolerate touching the clear vessel.

"If it's too disgusting, you don't have to warm it for me."

"For you, big boy, anything."

Did she wink at me? Is this happening? There was an old children's tale on Larian about monsters who came down from the mountains and stole children's souls, exchanging them for another's. The thought flies through my head that my kiss took Grace away and gave me someone else. But I like this new Grace. She's even more dazzling with a smile on her face.

She dishes some of the "sack of shit" as she calls it, onto a plate. "Enough?"

"More."

A few more spoonfuls. "Enough?"

"A little more."

She's almost emptied the container, so now she dumps the thing upside down and fills my plate until it's almost over-flowing. She places the plate in the heating machine and turns it on, then goes back to the cold box to rummage for something for herself.

"Kindapeanutbutter!" she exclaims as she holds aloft a con-tainer she found in the cupboard next to Maddie's fresh-ly-baked bread.

"Go get a chair from the other room," she orders, point-ing a knife covered with kindapeanutbutter at the dining area. I come back with two chairs, but she's already sitting cross-legged on the huge metal prep table in the middle of the kitchen with her sandwich on a little plate on her lap.

My heaping plate, with gravy dripping over the rim, is set at the edge, a knife and fork nearby.

She scoots to the far end of the square table, as far from me as possible. I blink several times. Is she having second thoughts? Did leaving her for a moment to get chairs from the other room change her mood?

"I can't even stand the smell of that, Tyree. You enjoy yourself. You might have to take a shower before I allow you back in my bed." Her eyes widen in surprise. "Whoops. Was that presumptuous of me? You *are* coming back to my room tonight, right?" She cocks her head in question.

"I'm eating every *dracking* bite of this sack of shit, and then I'd be happy to take a shower." I realize I'll need one to relieve myself—a couple of times—if I'm going to spend the night in her bed. The bed in which we just shared the most blazing kiss in the history of the universe. "Then I'd be happy to lie in bed with you, Grace. Maybe we'll even sleep." I smile and raise an eyebrow in innuendo.

To make sure she knows I didn't mean to pressure her, I use my fork to fling a small, unidentified, food-like object at her; I'd found it hidden in the gravy.

"Seriously? Are you starting a food fight? After midnight? In Maddie's kitchen?"

She darts off the table and seems to be on the hunt for something to throw at me. I had no idea what I'd started.

"I hate to waste food." She shrugs after not finding anything that fits her criteria. Just as I relax she comes up behind me and smashes something all over my face. I reach up to feel furrows of sticky stuff all over my cheek.

I'm up out of my seat and running after her before she could expect it. I smash my cheek against her face, squishing whatever it is all over her.

"Blech! I can't believe you did that, Tyree!"

"You started it!"

"_You_ started it! You forked me with sack of shit. That was unacceptable!"

She's laughing and licking the goop off her fingers. She finds a good fingerful and swipes a dollop on the tip of my nose.

"Kindapeanutbutter," she announces and immediately licks it off.

I'm struck by her warmth and her proximity. This new Grace is so lighthearted and fun. I want more of this. I never want her to disappear.

My mood has changed. My heart is clenching with the sweetest yearning. My hands are sticky and dirty and I don't care. I press them into her hair and pull her to me. I'm aware of the tacky feel and sweet smell of the goo, but then I'm totally consumed with Grace, her lips, her fragrance. I kiss her hard. I can't get enough.

"Dear Gods, Grace. You are the best thing that ever happened to me." I'm licking the gunk, trying to clear a pathway for more of the sensual kisses we shared on the bed. But the situation isn't cooperating. We're dirty and sticky, and I can see what Grace meant when she said the _sacru sheswah_ smelled awful.

I glance down and see her looking up at me. Her eyes are shining; are they swimming with unshed tears?

"Did I do something?" My heart stutters in my chest. I'd never want to hurt her.

"No, Tyree. You just spoke the nicest words anyone's ever said to me. It touched my heart."

I hug her and press my lips to hers, and then I can't contain my laughter. "Good thing there aren't any mirrors in here, Miss Kindapeanutbutter. Because we've created a massive mess. Not only are we filthy, this room is a disaster. Maddie will kill us."

She grabs my hand and swiftly kisses my sticky palm, then releases it just as fast. "Let's clean up and go back to my room for a shower."

We make short work of the kitchen as we silently clean. *Drackhead* is standing at full attention in my loincloth relentlessly teasing me with the idea that Grace just suggested we'd be showering together in a matter of moments. I try to keep my thoughts in check—not get my hopes up. *Drackhead* has other ideas.

Chapter Seven

GRACE

We ran back to my room giggling and holding hands. For the first time in my life, I can use the word "abandoned" to describe my behavior. Giggling! Really? I don't believe I've ever giggled in my life.

Tyree has peanut butter everywhere: smashed in his hair, drying on those long, pointed ears, plastered to his jumpsuit. I'm sure I'm just as bad. I press my palm on the plate to enter my room and see I've left a film of peanut butter in the shape of my hand. It strikes me as hilarious.

I grab some toilet paper, moisten it, and go out to wipe the plate down. When I return, I abruptly turn serious. Tyree is standing there, his hand on the autozip of his jumpsuit. He seems paralyzed. All of a sudden, I feel that way too.

Choice point. Big moment in Grace's life. Do I crawl back into my shell, take a quick solitary shower, then wait in bed while he takes his? Do I wait, projecting sensual videos of what's probably going on in the shower while I sit alone, my clit fluttering with desire? Or do I cross the threshold with him? Should I listen to the blood pounding in my veins, urging me to take a chance and follow my heart for once in my freaking life?

I think I might be the only woman I've ever met who would give this more than a cursory thought. No one else would agonize over this decision; they'd already be shucking their clothes and turning on the shower. But I'm still Grace. I need to think this through. I'd be stepping past another doorway through which I could never retreat. No going back after this.

I thought I'd go to my grave a virgin. I'd had no desire to lose myself to a man, to give up my autonomy like my mother did. But I'm not her. I have choices. I choose to follow my desires. I choose to march into the shower with Tyree.

"Let me help you with that, big guy." Grabbing his hand on the top of his zipper, I keep my voice light and breezy like we've been for the past hour, but it's a little strained.

His hand closes over mine, holding it in place as he spears me with a serious look. "You sure? We have all the time in the galaxy, Grace."

"I want to take a shower with you, Tyree. No guarantees implied or intended about anything that might or might not happen after that."

He smiles so slowly it seems to take a full minute from when the corners of his lips begin to lift to when his mouth is stretched into a full smile, happiness reaching his eyes.

"No pressure, Grace. We'll take this as slow as we want."

I remove my hands from his and move them to his shoulders, stepping closer, between his feet. I kiss him once, soft as a butterfly's wing. "Computer, dim lights."

My body's flat against his. I can feel his erection pressing against my abdomen. I can feel it pulse even through both sets of clothes. His breath hitches and he tilts his head back. I'm not just in the arms of a male. I'm in the arms of the most masculine male in the galaxy. I feel his muscular pecs under my fingers, his cock throbbing against me. I observe his head as it tips back, noticing the virile planes of his face, the hollows beneath his cheekbones.

My body is thrumming with desire, too. My clit is pulsing with need, my breath has quickened. I can't wait to touch his naked, bronze flesh.

"You smell like sack of shit, handsome. Let's waltz into the shower."

No waltzing for us. Hercules just bends down and lifts me in the bride-over-the-threshold grip like I weigh no more than a kitten. He walks us into the bathroom, turns on the water, then comes full stop. He looks at me, his gaze so fierce, so blazingly hot, I clutch his shoulders tighter, afraid I'll melt.

His eyes are kind and warm as he looks at me. I studiously avoid the mirror. I don't want to see the usual Grace: slightly awkward, no fashion sense, currently painted in peanut butter. I'd rather see myself through his eyes. And if the expression on his face is any indication, the view from Tyree's blazing green eyes is pretty spectacular.

Still in his arms, I accidentally catch a glimpse of myself in the mirror and can hardly recognize myself. My smile is loose and genuine, my eyes are glowing, happy. Uptight Grace has left the building and in her place is a new, calmer, happier version.

He gently sets me down, lifts the t-shirt over my head, and sucks in a quick intake of breath. "Grace, you are so beautiful. I've dreamed of this day. I've fantasized about you. I've imagined every *ince* of your skin. The reality of you is so much better than my daydreams could do justice."

He'll never figure out the clasp of my bra; I don't want to interrupt this moment. I undo it. As it slides to the floor I hear his muffled moan, which is answered by an echo of my own.

I never want to forget the look of hunger, of raw appreciation on his face. His hands are fisted at his sides. He's obviously using all his self-control not to attack me. My breathing is ragged from both fear and excitement, but I know one thing—I want to be naked in the shower with him—and soon.

His hands skim my leggings to the floor and I step out of them.

"A present," he breathes. "I'm unwrapping the best present of my life, Grace. You."

Wow. I never imagined a moment like this. But if I had, my fantasies could never have come close to this reality. At no time in my past did I believe I'd be precious to someone. My chest feels so full it could burst.

He strips off his jumpsuit and loincloth. In a hurry, I guess, to get in the shower. I drink in the sight of him. Struck again by the absolute beauty of his body. Perfection. His cock is huge, thick. It juts away from his body—proud and hard.

He moves us into the shower. It's a tight fit, maybe five feet by three feet. "Computer, lights out," he commands.

It's pitch black in here. Like being in a cave, deep underground. For a split second, I mourn the loss of my sight. I won't be able to see the water slide over him, won't be able to see the play of his muscles under his tan skin. Then I realize I can focus completely on my other senses. My clit pulses in anticipation.

He turns me toward the back of the shower, him standing between me and the spray of the water. He lifts my arms and places my palms on the wall

Pulling the shower head off its holder, he sprays me from the top of the head to my feet. The water is warm and would be soothing if I weren't already so ramped up with excitement.

"Face me," his voice is deep and commanding, brooking no argument. I have no intention to disobey.

I do as he says, and he sprays my hair so the water sluices down my back. I smell the kindapeanutbutter for a moment, then don't smell it anymore. It must all be washed down the drain. The warm water showers my shoulders and collarbones, then my breasts, midriff, thighs, and shins.

"Turn around, hands on the back wall again." He pauses, then, "Spread your legs." His voice is less than an inch from my ear. His warm breath fans my skin. That sexy command made my insides quake in anticipation.

His arm snakes around me, pulling my hips back toward him until my ass is presented to him. His foot nudges first my right foot, then my left farther apart. Even though the lights are off, I feel open, exposed. With my ass in this position, my balance is a little off, I feel slightly vulnerable, which ratchets up my desire. Although the tepid water's pounding down on me, it feels like hot tongues of fire are licking along my veins. I hear raspy breathing and realize it's mine. My mouth is open, I'm panting.

Tyree sprays my feet, my heels, and slowly the water moves up my inner thighs and finally onto my open slit.

I realize he hasn't touched me yet. He's simply given orders and sprayed water. Just with this, though, my arousal is off the charts.

I hear him place the showerhead in its holster, then search for something. Must have been looking for the shampoo because I hear the bottle being shaken, and the little gasp it makes when it releases product.

Now both his hands gently apply the shampoo to my shoulder-length hair. His fingers are slow and methodical, tenderly washing with care. The pads of his fingers are massaging my scalp. Part of me wants to melt into this relaxation, the other part is aware the pulsebeat of my heart is echoed in my clit. I want to be touched there by more than water.

We both simultaneously suck in a gasp of breath when his erect cock accidentally brushes my ass.

"Grace," he hisses.

He stills for a moment, then goes back to his ministrations with my hair. The juxtaposition of incongruity strikes me—his soft touch on my scalp, and what must be going on in his mind—because his cock is hard enough to hammer nails.

I can't bear it a minute more. I reach around to grab his erection. My hand just grazes it when I feel him jackknife back, out of my reach.

"Hands on the wall, Grace," his tone is commanding.

He sprays my hair; I can no longer smell the floral shampoo. Okay, Tyree. I certainly must be clean enough now. But no. He's found the soap and his hands are slippery with it when he lays them on my neck, then rubs. Strong fingers instinctively find the muscles near my shoulder blades that always carry my tension. Then his hands smooth the lather over my shoulders, down my arms; they slide to the incline of my waist, and then they still.

I'm totally focused on my senses right now. The splash of the water, the sound of his ragged breathing—and my own. But mostly, I'm aware of his hands on my hips. Touch me! I command in the silence of my mind. I press my ass back an inch. An invitation? Or an order to explore.

But instead, his deep voice commands, "Turn around." I comply.

Soaping his hands again, he starts at my collarbones, they slope to my shoulders, then down my arms, hips, and outer legs. I'm clean now, Tyree. Definitely clean enough!

"You've missed some spots," I chide. I'm dying. I want him to touch my breasts and nipples so badly I want to tug his hands there. But I wait. Obedient.

Finally, his hands move. I remember this is new to him, too. His voice sounded so confident, but are his hands trembling? They hold the weight of my breasts and he moans with pleasure. "I can picture these, Grace. Lovely, so full."

His thumbs flick the tips and I tilt my head back in pure pleasure. Catching the nubs between thumbs and forefingers, he presses and twists. A deep noise escapes the back of my throat as my hips press toward him. He continues for long moments until I'm moaning loudly and thrusting at empty air. I move toward him and hook one leg behind his thigh, trying to press my bundle of nerves against him, to feel some pressure

His hands leave my breasts and he hoists me up and closer to him. Yes, I'm riding his hip; I can feel his bone beneath my clit. The pressure is divine. His mouth is on my nipple now. He explores, first with the flat of his tongue, then the stiff tip, then the gentle scrape of his teeth.

Between the pressure on my clit and the attention to my nipples, I wonder if I could orgasm from this.

My breathing ramps faster. I snake one hand around his waist, then search for and find his cock with the other.

"Oh my God, Tyree." My voice is so low and breathy it sounds nothing like me. I'm on overload. Sensations coming at me from so many different directions, I'm glad there's nothing to look at. I have his cock in my fist, my fingers unable to meet. I can feel his blood pulsing under his skin.

"I want to taste you," we both say at the same time.

"Bed!" he commands. "Computer, dim lights." He turns off the water, slides me to the floor, opens the shower door, and grabs a white towel. He spears me with his molten gaze as he dries me with quick efficiency.

"I'm going to have my mouth on you in less than two *minimas*, Grace. If you don't want that, you have to tell me now. I'm on fire for you. I want to taste your cream. I want to hear you come."

"Yes. Yes. I've never been so ready." I explore my thoughts and feelings once more, searching for any part of me that isn't ready. Nope, I think all my multiple personalities are on board for whatever comes next—gee, I hope it's me!

Tyree

I take a few swipes at my skin with the towel and call it good, then I pick Grace up as if she's the most precious thing in the universe—she is. I lay her on the sheets and memorize the sight of her.

"You're the loveliest female I've ever seen. I want to pleasure you in every way imaginable. I want to make you happy, Grace."

I can't tell her I want her to be my mate. I can't tell her she's already my truemate—it would terrify her and make her doubt my true attraction—but I can treat her with all the affection and tenderness a male bestows upon his truemate.

I join her on the bed, and a bolt of worry slashes through me. I've never kissed anyone before today. I haven't been a sexual being for even one lunar cycle. I wonder if I'll know what to do, if I can please her, if I'm male enough or skilled enough.

Then I look at her naked body. I notice the pounding hunger thrumming through my veins. I connect with all the desire and devotion I have for her. I'll figure it out. We'll figure this out together.

I lie next to her and I kiss her, stroking her tongue with mine. My hands skim from shoulders to waist.

"I'm wet for you, Tyree. I want you."

She's ramped up. She needs no more foreplay. I move both knees between her legs and she opens herself to me. I catch the briefest peek before she tells the computer to turn the lights out. Better this way—we'll both just feel. I kiss from her navel to the patch of hair above her sex. I can smell her deep, musky arousal. My heart squeezes in my chest knowing her body is so ready for me.

I explore with my fingers, touching the small nub at the top of her cleft. This evokes a gasp and a roll of her hips. This is the button the males talk about, the spot the females like the best. I press and roll it, which garners moans of pleasure until she pulls away with an "ow."

Too hard, okay I got it. This is a better job for my tongue. I bend over and touch with the tip of my tongue. The hiss I hear and the way her muscles melt into the bed tells me I'm on the right track.

I swirl the little bud; she bucks her hips. I scoop my arms under her thighs; my hands on her hips so I have her pinned and can press my mouth against her as hard as she wants. But I have to taste her. My tongue follows her folds to her core and I stab into her. Dear Gods, she tastes so good. It is such a foreign flavor, and at the same time, it's like coming home.

Her fingers thread through my hair and she pushes me even deeper into her. I press my tongue as far into her channel as I can, and her hips roll again. She is chanting my name like it's a command—or a prayer. I'm trying to focus only on her, only on her pleasure, but *Drackhead* is frustrated and demanding release.

I move my mouth back to her nub and slide a finger into her wet channel. She lets loose a keening moan. I think she's incapable of speech. I press a bit harder with my tongue and her moan changes key. When I slip a second finger inside her, her noises intensify and she presses my head closer. "Tyree." If it wasn't my own name, I'm not certain I would understand it, it's so deep and distorted from her passion. Then her channel spasms around my fingers as her fingernails bite into my shoulders.

My releases usually last only a few moments, but hers seems to go on much longer. Her hips are writhing, words have escaped her and she's reduced to long, low wails. Finally, the muscles inside her channel slow their rhythm, then stop. She pulls me up until my head is near hers on the pillow. She kisses my face. Dozens of tiny, quick kisses—maybe hundreds.

"Tyree. Tyree. Amazing."

She's still panting. *Drackhead* is pulsing with need, more insistent than he's ever been. If I could extricate myself from her embrace, I could hurry into the bathroom to take care of myself so I can come back to bed and lay her head on my arm.

"Back in a moment. Computer, dim lights." I slide off the bed and hurry to the toilet. It's the work of a moment to take care of *Drackhead*.

"Tyree! Don't! I want to..."

"Tonight was about you, *Amara*," I explain as I saunter back into the room. "All you. Later, we'll do anything we've ever dreamed of with each other. Tonight you get to sleep. Need a treatment?"

"I think I just got a treatment, Tyree. I wanted to give you one," her voice is husky, but her face is calm. She's the happy Grace from the kitchen. Good. I don't want her having second thoughts.

"So sweet, so generous. I...will wait."

"What does *Amara* mean?"

"Everything. Every good and sweet thing a male can believe about his female. A term of affection, endearment." I climb into bed and scoot next to her, my weight on my hip, and kiss her lips sweetly, her nose, each eyelid. "It's how I feel about you, *Amara*."

She looks sated, happy. I love that I put that look on her usually-serious face. "Feel good?" I ask, attempting to hide the smug look that must be written all over my face.

She reaches over to kiss me. "You have to ask after that? Maybe I didn't scream loud enough. Perhaps Zar and Anya at the far end of the hall didn't hear us. Should we try again?"

"Tomorrow, *Amara*." I chuckle. Throwing my arm around her, I pull her on her side and nestle her back to my front. I kiss the nape of her neck gently. "Wake me if you get worried. Promise."

"Okay."

"Seriously, promise you will. I'll feel terrible if I wake up and find out you were miserable all night when I was only a heartbeat away."

"Okay. Promise."

Chapter Eight

TYREE

"Females and males," Zar's serious, hushed voice wakes me from sound sleep. "We've been halted by Federation command."

Every muscle in my body tightens, I pull Grace close, my eyes wide in fright despite the complete darkness.

"We've been ordered to nearby coordinates to wait to be boarded. I can only assume..." The speaker clicks off, then on again. "I can only assume we've been reported. We'll be at the checkpoint in less than fifteen *minimas*. I recomme nd...you say your goodbyes to anyone you hold dear...," his voice is choked.

I hear footsteps pounding down the hallway. I don't need telepathy to see in my mind's eye males running to their females' rooms.

"*Amara*." My heart is clenching with emotion.

She flips on her side to face me. "Computer, dim lights," she orders as she presses her palm to my cheek. Her blue eyes are rounded in fear as she searches my face. I see her terror increase as she sees the alarm in my expression.

"It's happening," she whispers. "I never thought it would. What will they do to us?"

"There's no way to know for certain. The best-case scenario would be for us all to be sold. The worst-case…?" my words drop off. She doesn't need to hear it, I'm certain her thoughts have already flown to many worst-case scenarios.

"Kidnapping is illegal. You and I were kidnapped from our home planets. Wouldn't they let us go?" Her voice holds hope. I hate to dash it, but she shouldn't cling to false hope, better she begin to prepare for her new reality.

"Our planets know nothing of other beings in the galaxy, the Federation would never return us to our homes. It's why you females decided you could never return to Earth. Chaos would break out if the existence of alien species was confirmed."

"So they'd let us go to a safe planet? Be free?"

"Perhaps on your planet the rulers are benevolent and altruistic, my *Amara*, but the Federation isn't like that. I imagine they'll sell us." I want to add that we'll be separated, but she's smart enough to know we'll never be kept together.

She leans to kiss me. This isn't one of the tender kisses she's so fond of. This kiss is fierce. It's a message. It's as if she wants to mark me with her essence, her entire being.

Grace

What they say about time slowing down in a crisis is true. Suddenly all the questions and confusion that's been spinning in my head grind to a halt. I have true clarity for the first time since my kidnap—maybe for the first time in my life.

"Time is short, Tyree." I spear him with a hard gaze, willing him to know just exactly how serious I am. "Make love to me."

If I'm going to be dragged off this ship and away from this male, I want his essence inside me. Part of my brain is shocked at this primitive urge which rose from some primal reflex that's lain dormant inside me. "Make love to me," I repeat as I move down his body to lick his cock to convince him.

That wasn't necessary, he's already stiff and ready for me. At least his body is.

"Are you sure, Grace? The timing…"

"If I never see you again, I want to have this memory. Forever."

I doubt I'm wet enough to receive him. I'm not aroused. This is a need more primitive than sex. It's deeper than that. It's life and death.

"Females and males," Zar's voice interrupts, "we've arrived at our coordinates. There are five other vessels in line ahead of us at this checkpoint. I'll keep you informed."

I don't have time to process what his words mean other than to feel a modicum of relief as I realize this gives Tyree and me more time for this. I still feel the urgency to couple with him, to have part of him inside me.

Tyree rolls on top of me, his knees straddling my hips, his elbows near my shoulders, his eyes speaking volumes to mine.

His kisses morph from the hard claiming kisses we were just sharing to tender expressions of his emotions.

He leans down and whispers in my ear, "can I tell you, *Amara?* Can I tell you what I've always known?" His fingers spear into my hair and he pulls me so close his lips touch the shell of my ear. "You're my truemate, Grace. I've known almost since we met that you're my female. I Transformed for you. My body knows yours, *Amara.* I think your body knows mine, too."

My head is spinning with this information, yet in the back of my mind I've often wondered. His body needed a truemate to transform and here we are. If he didn't transform for me, then who?

He sits up to look at me. I know he's memorizing every curve and plane of my face and body, just as I'm memorizing him. He smiles at me; it's reassuring and shocking at the same time. Our lives could be over in less than an hour and yet we have this, this precious connection that can't be severed. I smile back at him.

He plucks my nipples, then bends his blond head and scrapes the tips. This isn't what either of us wanted for our first time. Like a death-row prisoner's last meal, there's really no way it can be savored.

He moves his knees between my own, then slides his fingers into my folds. Impossibly, I must be wet for him, as I feel him glide from clit to core. I hear my quick intake of breath. Surreal how the body can respond, even in a moment like this.

"This is what you want, *Amara*?"

My answer is to grasp his cock and stroke it, then move it toward my entrance.

The words "I love you" are pounding in my thoughts, but I think the timing would cheapen them. I'll tell him in a moment.

He presses into me gently, his eyes never leaving mine. This isn't sexual passion—nothing like that. It's the connection of souls.

His thrusts are slow and deep and serious. Every drive of his hips speaks volumes of words we've never exchanged.

I don't find release, I didn't expect to—don't desire it. I wanted more than that. I wanted the connection.

He orgasms deep inside me, then turns us on our sides to face each other, still connected.

"Our souls just joined, *Amara*. They can't part us now. If we're separated here, I'll find you in the afterlife. I swear that, Grace. My thoughts will never leave you. I will never leave you."

One of my hands is stroking his back from shoulder to hip. The knuckles of my other hand are brushing his cheek.

I guess I could die now if the Federation wants to kill me. Something's changed in me. I've faced death and accepted it.

"I—" I begin.

"Females and males," Zar's voice interrupts. His tone sounds completely different. "We've been given permission to be on our way. Evidently, they found whoever they were looking for and apprehended them. I for one can't wait to get to Emirus and get our papers in order. That just took ten years off my life."

Grace

Tyree and I didn't say much after our close call last night. Between the adrenaline overload and my shock at my own behavior, I was pretty preoccupied.

I'm in his arms, wrapped tight and secure with all the love he shared with me last night, yet my thoughts are spinning with worry.

I always knew I had this performance phobia, I tried to fix it with therapy and meds with no success. But it's at this very moment I realize how fucked up I am in other ways. Instead of basking in the protective embrace of the galaxy's sweetest male, I'm frantic with terror at being emotionally close.

My mind is bombarding me with pictures from my childhood, and none of them are good. I'm remembering all the ways my mom gave away big gobs of herself to the men in her life—and how she risked my safety as well—just to have a man at her side.

I don't want to lose myself. I know I'm not my mom. I'm not addicted to meth or crack or opioids. But she was also addicted to men. She couldn't tolerate us being a little family—just her and me. She always had to have some guy around, no matter how broke or mean or controlling he was. I promised myself years ago I'd never need anyone. Even now, even though Tyree has been nothing but nice to me, I don't want to need him.

He poured out his heart to me last night. He admitted I'm his truemate. At the time I believed he was mine as well. How do I tell him I changed my mind?

I don't want to break his heart, especially since I'm so confused. A tiny modicum of peace washes over me as I realize I don't have to do anything right now.

I'm going to kiss his sweet, bronzed cheek and get up and do what needs to be done. I have a concert tomorrow and I need to get ready. Nothing needs to be discussed or decided today. I don't need to figure this out right now.

Today's agenda is to practice my ass off and make sure I've got my program down pat. I can already feel my performance anxiety escalating. It hovers near the edge of my consciousness—little swells of worry, an electric tightness that zips along my veins and nerve endings. Just yanking my chain a little bit, reminding me it's there—it hasn't disappeared.

For some reason, even though his eyes are closed, I know Tyree's awake. That's okay. I watch him, inspect that flawless face of his. Straight nose, strong chin, sexy ears, beautiful bronze skin. Lips that are totally masculine—and kissable.

I scoot even closer, put my arm around him and press my lips to his. Just once, soft and sweet.

His eyes pop open and his mouth turns up in a slow smile. He pulls me even closer. Without thinking, I sling my leg over his. Now my core is open to him and pressed against his pulsing erection.

"Whoops." I pull my leg back to where it was.

"Yes," he agrees, "whoops. You have rehearsing to do. I do, also. I'm going to Emirus with you, as part of your guard. I've been practicing various martial arts techniques since my Transformation, but today I want to make certain I'm fully trained on the gun I'll be taking down to the planet."

"Guard? Gun?"

"Didn't Captain Zar inform you? You've been so worried about your concert that you've given no thought to the fact that you'll be on an unknown planet. Totally exposed. We've been planning for your safety since we agreed to the contract.

"The women will stay on the ship, but six gladiators will accompany you to Emirus. The males have been sewing their uniforms for the past few days. You're going to have an impressive entourage that screams to anyone who's watching that they shouldn't *drack* with you."

"Great, something new to worry about."

"I told you all this to *relieve* your worries, *Amara*. The gladiators will keep you safe." He kisses my nose, then pulls back and glances at my computer. "There's a message flashing, Zar wants you to stop by Savannah's cabin. Something about a gown."

We get dressed and go our separate ways; I have so much to do today. Good. That will keep me from worrying about my relationship with Tyree.

Stopping by the dining room to grab some breakfast, I notice some peanutbuttery prints on the prep table legs. I clean up before Maddie sees, she's a stickler for a clean kitchen. I make a quick sandwich and eat it on the run to Savannah's cabin.

"That was quite a scare last night," Savannah expels a long, deep sigh.

"Yeah, amazing that the galactic equivalent of a routine traffic stop could turn everyone's lives upside down like that."

"Theos and I thought we were all dead."

"Tyree and I were saying our goodbyes," I admit.

"I imagine everyone was. Close call, huh? It just reminds you that we have to live in the moment."

I nod, but in the back of my mind I admit to myself I'm incapable of that.

"You know I ordered you three dresses, right?" Savannah asks, changing the subject. She's wearing cargo pants and a t-shirt, her usual no-nonsense, military self.

"Um, no."

"Yeah. My marine side is kinda balanced out by my girly side. I don't know what I miss most about Earth—my target practice or my monthly subscription to fashion magazines." She gives me a sly smile. "I poured over the Intergalactic Database's equivalent of *Vogue* and ordered you a gown for each night."

"Gowns?" The fanciest thing I've ever worn in my life was a $50 recital dress from Forever 21. "What do you mean when you say gown?"

She stalks over to her computer, pulls up a picture and motions me over. The dress is white and silky and like something out of a fairytale.

"That's for me?" I sound breathless.

"Zoey still had your measurements from our excursion to Numa when we bought new clothes. This was ordered just for you."

Something doesn't feel right—like a circuit disconnect. That dress? On that screen? Is for me?

"I ordered you one for each night." She pulls up two more pics: one is ruby red, the other is the exact emerald green of Tyree's eyes. All three gowns are very similar styles—fancy and gorgeous.

"Wow, I don't know what to say. I'll feel like a queen. Thanks."

"I knew you were in no shape to be looking through catalogs the day this happened and we needed a quick turnaround. I thought I knew your taste. I've watched you since the revolution. I knew you'd want to be modest and feminine. I think they'll fit you perfectly." She's beaming. "You'll look even more lovely than usual when you're wearing one of these."

"Looks like you spent a fortune," I still can't believe these beautiful creations are for me. And did she just say I was lovely? It must be backward day.

"Leaving you out of the loop gave us more time and allowed me to order these handmade from what must be an inter-galactic knockoff factory. They're reproductions at about ten cents on the dollar. I've been in contact with them daily, and I'm assured they'll all be ready in time for your first performance." She pauses, then, "Maybe I should have put you in the loop, Grace. I just wanted everything to go off without a hitch...and I loved looking at all the pretty dresses."

"You can have them all in four days. I can't imagine I'll ever wear them again."

"You're going to do fine, you know. Your music is amazing."

"Thanks, Savannah, but hearing it and believing it are two different things." I pause, then grab her hand. "I'm nervous and scared, but I need to step up, put on my big girl panties, and do us all proud." She smiles at me. "Oh, speaking of which, you didn't happen to order any underwear, did you?"

"You won't need a bra. The dresses themselves do all the heavy lifting. And yes, I ordered panties for every woman on this ship. We deserve it, and even if the guys find out, I don't believe one of them will complain."

"You're right. None of the horny guys on the ship are going to gripe about their women having sexy underwear." I walk to the door, trying to get used to the idea of wearing those fancy dresses. "Thanks, Savannah."

Tyree

"Tyree and Grace, could you come to the bridge, please?" Captain Zar's voice booms over the loudspeaker.

Captain Zar, Callista on comms, and Axxios, the pilot, are on the bridge when I arrive. Grace appears a moment later.

"Thanks for coming, have a seat. I trust you're all recovering from last night's close call." Then Zar gets down to business, "Callista gathered some intel I wanted to review with you before we hit atmo on Emirus."

I sit in my first mate chair while Grace grabs a spot on one of the small jumpseats ringing the back wall. I can tell she's nervous and seems to want no part of this briefing.

I calm her from here. I don't even close my eyes; I just push a gust of serenity at her. I see her shoulders relax. I blast her with another round and see her take in a full breath. She glances over at me and smiles.

"Callista? Go ahead."

"The MarZan cartel has definitely intensified their search for us in the last few days. Not only did we disable their ship the other night, I wonder if they figured out it was us on Ortheon II a month ago when Shadow and Petra killed two MarZan operatives on their mission to the surface.

"I've been picking up space chatter between MarZan ships several times a day. They're on the hunt for us in a big way. Seems we provoked the head of the syndicate, Daneur Khour, and he doesn't like to lose face. Or money. Or possessions, which is what we are to him. Not to mention this vessel.

"So far, I've heard absolutely nothing about Emirus. I don't believe they've linked the concert to us. But I know this is an important mission, and I wanted to make sure everyone was apprised of this status."

"So, nothing in particular to worry about. Just something to keep in mind. Thanks, Callista. Good work." Zar nods at her. It often strikes me that although he's the least humanoid in appearance of anyone on board, with his feline features and furred body, he's one of the strongest, most compassionate males I've ever met. He's taken on a lot. From being born a slave to leading an insurrection with his mate, Anya, to captaining this ship. I have tremendous respect for him.

"Shadow's been trying his hand at a lot of jobs around the ship since he decided he wants no part of the gladiator's life. I tasked him with looking into Argento Quirinus, the Emperor.

"He briefed me on some information I thought you should know. This is not a democratic planet but is ruled by the royal family, of which Quirinus is the head. The planet is well run with little petty crime, few murders, and clean streets. And before you decide this sounds like a good place to move, what it really means is that the citizens are terrified of their leader and walk the straight and narrow under fear of severe punishment.

"That's about all we know. It sounds like this mission should be a quick in and out. You'll have a solid gladiatorial guard, including Shadow."

"But I thought he didn't want to...," Grace interjects.

"He demanded to go," Zar answers. "Said he wouldn't hear of Grace or Tyree going to the planet surface without his personal protection. I'm certain you'll all be fine." He pauses, then, "As long as you don't spit on the street. It's a punishable offense. Don't sit before the Emperor is seated. If he invites you to dine with him don't eat before he does, and don't stop until he pushes his silverware into the middle of his plate."

"Punishable offenses?" Grace asks, eyes wide in fright.

"Punishable offenses," Zar nods. "Thanks for coming."

"Can I get up now, or is that a punishable offense?" Grace jokes.

"You'll do fine down there. We get there by lunchtime to-morrow. Savannah suggested that Petra should accompany you, to do...let me check my notes, hair and makeup. You'll pick up your gowns and do any last-minute alterations, then arrive at the concert hall by 1830. The performance starts at 2000."

Chapter Nine

GRACE

I wake the next day, my skin covered in a thin sheen of perspiration. I was having the naked performance dream again. Enough of this shit! I don't have time for anxiety.

I run at top speed all morning, taking care of loose ends. At one point I realize all I have for shoes is a pair of crappy alien flip flops, but Savannah assures me she's found a store on Emirus near the dress shop.

Finally, I'm waiting at the ramp to leave, my two instruments carefully wrapped in a large roller bag which Petra kindly takes control of. Tyree's there looking handsome in his new uniform with his chainsticks and laser on his belt. The males could all be mistaken for Chippendale models with their muscular physiques, black leather kilt-like bottoms, and black sash-covered chests. They look imposing—and like an efficient machine.

"All this for me?" I whisper to Tyree.

"It seems you're famous now, *Amara*. Crazy things happen. We want to make certain you're protected."

"Can I have your attention?" Zar's sonorous voice intrudes over the cacophony of voices in the small exit area we're crammed into. "Doctore and Stryker, you're going to accompany Maddie to the mercantile and back as she picks up supplies. When she's safely back here you'll proceed to the concert hall to wait for the others. I'd like you to check out the hall itself, and the room where Grace will be housed prior to and after the performance. I want this to go off without any problems.

"Shadow's in charge of this mission, I want you all to report to him. He'll make all decisions on the ground. Theos, Dax, Steele, and Tyree will accompany Grace and Petra on their shopping trip, then to the concert hall. No extra stops. The concert hall will be easier to defend than any random street corner. Are we clear?"

"Is this really necessary?" I ask.

"Callista's been monitoring comms. Sounds like off-worlders are pouring in from every corner of the galaxy for the concert. Scalpers are selling tickets for over five thousand credits apiece. We just want to keep you safe."

My knees actually buckle. I would have hit the floor if Tyree hadn't caught me under my arm and held me up.

"Shadow, keep me informed at thirty *minima* intervals," Zar says. "Be safe out there."

My guards form a phalanx around me, except for Tyree who stays at my side, one hand respectfully but firmly under my arm.

With over a thousand pounds of well-armed muscle surrounding me, it takes a moment for me to see what awaits us outside our vessel. My feet barely touch the tarmac when I see hundreds of aliens of all sizes, shapes, and colors. Some are behind ropes; those must be civilian onlookers. But there are dozens of beings inside the ropes, many taking pictures with tiny devices. Some are shouting questions at me as they press closer.

I feel Tyree tense beside me. "Can you walk under your own steam, Grace? I'd rather have both hands free to protect you." His eyes are scanning the environment for threats.

I nod and move away from him, walking on my own steam. *Okay, Grace, this is the moment of truth. You need to pull yourself together*, I scold myself. I flash pictures on the mental screen inside my head—dozens of them. Times when I found my own inner strength and took care of myself. I straighten my spine, ball my hands into fists, and lift my chin.

I can do this. Dealing with Barbarian was harder than this. Calling 911 at age six when my mom overdosed and passed out on the bathroom floor in a pool of her own vomit was harder than this. Coping with the kids at school making fun of me because I smelled like dirty laundry was harder than this.

Fuck you! I think. Fuck you all. I can do this!

My spine is ramrod straight as I step forward. I'm going to meet an Emperor today. But I'm a queen, I tell myself. I'm a fucking queen, and they can all kiss my ass. I'm going to play music the angels would be jealous of. People are paying five thousand credits a ticket to hear my music. And I'm worth it.

The gladiators protecting me are all vigilant. I can see their tight muscles; they all have both hands on their weapons.

"Out of the way!" Shadow orders the onslaught of reporters as we move to the waiting hovercraft.

"I had no idea..." I breathe when we're zipping through the streets of Almering toward the dress shop.

"I knew you were popular," Shadow says, "but I didn't know the crowd would look like that. I'm going to have Callista comm the Emperor's staff and see if we can have reinforcements meet us at the shop and stay with us through your entire engagement on Emirus. There must have been a hundred reporters swarming us. This is a circus."

Our hovercraft is speeding fast, like we're on some important mission rather than going to a dress shop. I sneak peeks at the scenery out my side window. The Database said there were over twelve million people in this city, but it seems almost like a small town. Street after street with shops at street level and living spaces up above. Everything seems immaculate. I guess that's what happens when you're ruled by a despot who forbids spitting and littering.

When I get a glance through the front window I'm struck by two things: the pink sky (how'd I miss that when I stepped out of our vessel?) and tall buildings up ahead. They look hundreds of stories high. We must have landed in the burbs and are now traveling toward the city proper.

The dress shop had already closed its doors to the public, so it's just the gladiators, Petra, and me in the small fabric-strewn space. It's maybe thirty by thirty feet, the floor is grimy, but the dresses hanging on racks in every available space look like the most glorious things I've ever seen.

The staff is comprised of four spindly humanoid females with elongated faces. Their skin seems to be stretched too tightly over protruding cheekbones. I have no idea about intergalactic fashion trends, but one sports a lime green wig, one is neon pink, one fire-engine red, and the other is cotton-candy blue.

Their fingers are long and slim. Perfect, I guess, for seamstresses. The three dresses Savannah ordered are hanging neatly over a three-way mirror. My breath gusts out in a huff of surprise when I see them. I've certainly never worn anything so fine or fancy.

There's a private room in the back for me to try them on. My image looks so foreign to me, it's hard to register what I really look like as I'm helped into the first one. Blood red, it's some type of material that feels softer than silk.

"Grace, you look hot," Petra says, then licks her finger, presses it to her hip and makes a sizzling sound. "Amazing."

I look more feminine than ever in my life. The waist is nipped, the hips are accentuated, and the color brings out my features. But the neckline is way too low. If I take a deep breath my areolas will show.

"Beautiful, ladies," I inform the seamstresses who all seem to wait breathlessly for my pronouncement. "Can we...add some lace here?" I point to the decolletage.

"But that's the style, Madam. And it looks so lovely on you." The one with the lime green wig informs me.

"Right you are," I tell her. "But I want to show less. Would lace work or do you have another idea?"

The four women put their heads together, then lime green shows me some black lace and tells me this will look attractive. We'll use the black lace retrofit for the red and green, white lace for the white dress—all will be done within an hour.

It's like that scene in *Pretty Woman* with all of them kissing my ass—so courteous and concerned about my every want and need. I've decided to just enjoy my little moment of fame. It will be the first and last time in my life I'm treated with this much deference.

Petra informs me we won't have to leave the dress shop to look for shoes; they've hauled in a variety in my size from the store down the street.

I'm still wearing the emerald green dress, as we search for appropriate shoes. I need a pair that is the right fit, the right height and, most importantly, doesn't have heels so high that I fall over when I walk.

If I wasn't already embarrassed about the excess boobage spilling out the top of the dress, the look on Tyree's face would push me over the edge. I've never seen him in this particular shade of red. His face is pinched in anger as he tries to keep his massive body between me and the gladiators so they don't get a chance to ogle me.

I glance out the storefront windows and glimpse what looks like hundreds of onlookers pressing toward the glass. "Um, guys, could the weight of all of those people actually break the glass?"

The males follow my gaze and see the crush of people. Some of their features are distorted because folks from behind are pressing so hard they're being smashed against the window.

"Tyree, Dax, you stay here and guard her. Theos and Steele, come with me, we've got to break this up," Shadow orders. "For *drack's* sake, get her out of sight."

Tyree and Dax hustle Petra and I into the windowless fitting room. The males have both drawn their guns and are on high alert. I have no idea what's happening outside this room, but I'm waiting to hear the sound of the huge plate glass windows splintering at any moment.

"Ladies," Dax calls to the seamstresses in the tiny adjoining sewing room. How do they even work in there? They're elbow to elbow, colorful heads bent low over their work. "Is there a back entrance to this shop?"

Cotton candy blue points to the back wall behind her. We'd have to move four chairs, four women, and two sewing machines to be able to open the door.

"If we hear glass break, we'll be forcing through that door," Dax informs them. "Best to get out of our way."

Luckily, moments later we're joined by Shadow and his men. "The Emperor's guards have arrived. They managed the crowd. We're fine." He looks shaken—lips pulled down in a scowl, swallowing hard.

"What happened out there?" Tyree asks.

"Brutal. Shock sticks. Many of the soldiers were on *mronckback* and used the animals to push the crowd down the street. At least five were trampled and badly hurt by my count. It was just an eager crowd. They wanted a glimpse of Grace, they're calling her 'Musician of Angels.'"

"People were hurt? Trying to see me?" My panic hits in full force. It's mingled with something else. Guilt? My chin quivers and I take a deep breath.

"It's not your fault," Shadow tells me. "You certainly didn't ask for this."

The ladies finish the dresses one by one. As soon as I try one on to make sure the lace looks right, they present me with the next. The gowns are wrapped as if they're precious jewels, then we're off to the concert hall in our hovercraft, surrounded by five similar craft holding over a hundred of the Emperor's soldiers.

Tyree

I can't wait until we're safely in the concert hall. Grace is far too exposed and vulnerable as we move her through the city. Luckily this vehicle's windows are obscured, so no onlookers can see Grace's lovely face pressed against the glass as she gawks at the sights.

"Oh my gosh. That building has to be three hundred stories high." Her mouth is actually gaping open in awe. "Is it peaking above the clouds? And the pink sky! I can't get over it."

Even though we're surrounded by soldiers as well as our own gladiatorial guards, I stay attentive. That said, I can't help occasionally glancing out the windows myself. I've been a slave for a long time, either kept underground in a cell, on board a ship, or as a house pet. My home planet's major mode of transportation was *ortoni*-drawn wagons. We had no structures higher than three stories. I must admit I'm fascinated by what I see whizzing by these windows.

At last, we pull up to the concert hall, which occupies an entire city block. I look over at Grace and see her swallow several times as she absorbs the enormity and scope of the building. To compare it to a palace would be a disservice. It's incredible.

I keep myself focused on the business at hand, reminding myself that my primary mission is Grace's safety. The other males are highly-trained gladiators. Until recently I was tripping over my own feet, still getting used to my new size. Despite that, I have an important job here. I need to protect her, preserve her safety, and keep her calm enough to perform.

Grace

The concert hall is like nothing I've ever seen before. I visualize pictures from the Internet of the enormous marble government buildings in Washington, D.C. Then times it by ten or maybe one hundred in terms of grandeur and expense. The design of the building is timeless; the gleaming columns of red and blue polished stone are breathtaking.

I was so consumed by the sights of Almering I got distracted. But now that we're parked at the concert hall my anxiety spirals. I take a deep breath, pull both hands to my sides, straighten my back and sweep into the huge anteroom, trying for all the world to act like a queen.

The foyer walls are azure blue, the doorways are burnished wood, and the ceiling is painted in intricate detail to resemble the pink skies of Emirus.

Everything else is gold. To my untrained eye, it is not gold paint or gold leaf or some fake metal. I believe every fixture, every knob and every kick plate on every door is real gold. I'm certain the cost of one doorknob alone could house a family of four on Earth for a year.

Mauritious introduces himself as the head of the palace guard. His navy-blue uniform is covered with enough gold buttons, gold epaulets, and gold braid for five generals' uniforms back home.

He sweeps us through the next set of doors into the concert hall itself. To see this place, knowing I'm going to perform here in a matter of hours makes my breath catch in my throat. I pause, not breathing for a moment, then my heart hammers in triple time.

I reach toward Tyree and the backs of my fingers unobtrusively brush his. I'd love a treatment right now, but barring that, just the physical connection will do. A gust of his compassionate calm presses into me. It races along my synapses, relaxing my thoughts as well as my muscles.

"Thank you, Tyree," I whisper. "I'm on overload."

"I don't blame you, Grace. It's pretty overwhelming for a poor boy from Larian as well."

Calm enough to really absorb what I'm observing, I pay attention to the enormity of this place. The word huge doesn't do it justice. The size of the hall boggles the mind.

"Six thousand seats on the main floor and the three balconies," Mauritious intones. "Another five hundred in the private boxes. And there," he indicates with an arrogant thrust of his fingers, "is His Majesty, Emperor Quirinus' private suite."

I keep my mouth from flopping open in awe as I take everything in. From the plush blood-red seats and curtains to the most beautiful, intricately-painted mural of what looks like a pantheon of Emirusian Gods on the domed ceiling, everything is exquisite.

Mauritious stops in front of me, bows low, his long black braid almost sweeping the floor, then stands in front of me and clicks his heels. "His Majesty asked me to invite you to his suite to share an aperitif with him an *hoara* before your show."

"I'm honored, sir." I don't think I've ever stretched my spine so straight or tipped my chin so arrogantly high. "I'm afraid I sequester myself into my private quarters prior to a performance. I meditate and commune quietly with my thoughts so that I may give a performance that will please the angels themselves. I must humbly decline his Majesty's most generous offer."

My heart is about to beat out of my chest. I just turned down the ruler of an entire freaking planet. Where did I find the nerve?

Mauritious' head rocks back in shock, his nostrils flaring, then he resumes his rigid posture. "I understand. You must prepare to entertain a discerning crowd of sixty-five hundred. I will tell the Emperor you've graciously declined."

Is he trying to intimidate me? He did a great job.

"When we spoke with your manager, we were under the impression you would be sleeping on your vessel each night," Mauritious says. "Might I suggest a change of plans? There are attached quarters off the rear of the building. Miss Grace, if you wish to utilize this it would be easier to ensure your safety and allow you to avoid trips back and forth through crowded streets. There are four sleeping rooms. They are adequately appointed—nothing fancy. I do not mean to insult you with the accommodations. I simply offer it as an option."

I look toward Tyree, then Shadow, frowning in confusion.

"Thank you so much, Captain Mauritious," Shadow says. "You've been very helpful. I believe we misjudged Grace's popularity. The level of difficulty with crowd control took us by surprise. Might I inspect the area?" Shadow asks politely. I forgot that before he became a gladiator he rubbed elbows with presidents and kings.

He returns a few minutes later. "It looks safe and solves the problem of transporting you to the ship and back each day. I suggest we take the captain up on his generous offer."

We hurry about half a city block through an underground walkway, to our appointed rooms. It's just as Mauritious described, a small living area attached to four separate bedrooms, each with their own bath. Tyree swiftly inspects all of them and chooses the slightly nicer, slightly larger one for me, for us.

After Mauritious and the guards leave, I sit heavily on the edge of a couch, Tyree joins me. We're so close our thighs touch.

"I imagine on a planet like this," Shadow says, "no matter how welcoming the head of state or Captain of his Guard is, that traveling musicians and their gladiatorial escort are considered riffraff. If I were in charge, I'd have cameras placed strategically around to make sure no one walks off with a golden doorknob or two."

I snort quietly, realizing I wasn't the only one to have that idea.

"I would assume we're being watched—everywhere."

I groan. This means I won't be able to fully put my guard down.

"Everything will work out." Tyree gives me a piercing look and then blasts a gust of calm at me.

Petra makes sure the gowns are hanging straight on a clothes rack before organizing the makeup and hair products on the dressing table in my room. Someone suggests I might want to take a nap. I would like nothing better, I got very little sleep last night and my nerves are frazzled.

I glance at Tyree, silently requesting he accompany me. He quickly stands and helps me up. "I've been your personal bodyguard since you needed one, milady. I wouldn't think of leaving you alone on this of all days," he says, loud enough for any microphones that might be listening.

Okay, so that's the cover story, he's my personal protector and doesn't leave my side. I don't know how we're going to manage the sleeping arrangements, but at least he's not expected to leave me at any time.

"As usual, my lady, I'll sleep on the floor near you, should you need me."

"Of course." I hope he can see my lips purse at the thought he would have to debase himself like that. "My ever-faithful servant, Tyree." Okay, maybe we can have some fun with this. Don't couples back on Earth role-play all the time? Well, instead of the French maid with her short skirt and feather duster, we have the hunky personal gladiator in his leather kilt at my beck and call. We'll make this work.

Tyree performs his magic from his blanket-covered spot on the floor, and I'm asleep before I know it. I wake to Petra's soft knock. "Grace, let's get you beautiful. If we start now, you'll have time for at least some tea and a delicious pastry the Emperor sent over for us. That is," she raises her voice so everyone in the suite can hear, "if the gladiator hordes haven't eaten every freaking one of them before you get a chance!"

"We can ask for more, Pet," I hear Shadow call from the common area around what sounds like a huge bite of food. "They're the best thing I've eaten since I was a free male on Morgana."

"Even though I love you and Grace forgave you, you're still a dick."

"You wound me," Shadow jokes as he stands in our doorway. He clamps a partially-eaten scone between his lips then places both hands on his chest and acts as if he's just been shot in the heart.

As Petra slips between him and the doorjamb to leave, he playfully slaps her ass.

"Keep that up big guy and I'll put you on restriction."

"Restriction from what?"

"You have many favorite pastimes, Shadow, and they all involve me. Use your imagination." She gives him a quelling look.

"My lady," Tyree says, "I agree with Petra that you should try to get a little food down. Do you want a pastry, or would you prefer a sandwich?"

"I know my stomach, Tyree. Thanks, but no food until after the performance. Tea sounds good, though."

Chapter Ten

GRACE

I know I'm twenty-six, but I can't help swaying in front of the mirror like a little girl in her first fancy dress. Petra did my hair in what she calls a "simple chignon." It's a fancy, slightly messy style pulled back in a low bun. Between the dress, the hair and the great job she did on my makeup, I find it hard to tear my eyes from the mirror.

I never wanted to attract attention to myself. As a young woman, I didn't experiment with makeup or hair. I either wear my hair down or pull it into a ponytail without benefit of looking in a mirror. In my head, I always described my looks as "okay." I would never use the words cute, pretty, or attractive.

But now, looking in the mirror, I've got to admit the word "pretty" wouldn't be too much of a stretch.

I'm wearing the green gown. It's the exact emerald color of Tyree's eyes, and of the three, I think it looks best on me—I really need my confidence tonight. First of all, there are sixty-five hundred patrons out there who will be scrutinizing me. Second, the Emperor of the entire freaking planet will be in his box watching me. Third, Shadow recently informed me that Emperor Quirinus apologized for his faux pas of inviting me for an aperitif before my program, and offered dinner afterward in his private suite.

I don't know how to weasel my way out of this. No pressure!

"All you have to do is slip on your shoes and you're ready to go," Petra pulls me out of my fear-induced reverie. "You look beautiful. Ready?"

I glance in the full-length mirror one more time. "I look...good. Thanks, Petra. You worked a miracle!"

"You're so pretty, Grace. You didn't need a miracle worker. You have great bone structure. Let's get a move on." She motions toward the door.

I take one last look in the mirror and have a quick internal fight with myself. The little girl inside thinks all everyone will see is the fifth-grader who wore smelly clothes to school. The grown-up Grace can see what I really look like in this exquisite green dress. The deciding factor will be the look on Tyree's face, although I know in my heart he thinks I'm attractive in anything I wear. And especially when I'm wearing nothing at all.

The hem of the dress is so wide I have to squish it through the doorway. The males are out in the hall, half looking one way, half looking the other—all on high alert. I hear crowd noises from the auditorium, even though we're several long hallways from there. Soft music is drifting in, maybe there's an orchestra playing as people take their seats. For some reason, the sound of the crowd is the thing that amps my anxiety into overdrive. Everything just got real.

Where is Tyree? I frantically look around for a moment, then see his broad back, flashes of his bronze skin peeking out from behind the strip of leather crossing his back. Then perhaps he feels my eyes on him and turns almost in slow motion.

The expression on his face when he sees me is a moment I want to keep in my mental photo album until my dying day. His face is at first impassive, then his eyes widen as he sees me. Almost like a double-take, he glances down to my shoes and up to my hair one more time. Then it's like he's convinced himself it's really me and his mouth turns into a grin that stretches wider and wider.

'Wow,' he mouths, then "Wow," he says more loudly. "Grace you look...what's the best word in your language? I want to get it right. What would be the most beautiful word in the Earth language?"

"Gorgeous," Petra offers. "Or Exquisite. Try Exquisite."

I don't know what word actually comes out of his mouth. It doesn't sound like English, nor does it translate from Larian. But the look on his face says all I need to hear. My stomach tightens, my clit pulses, and rivers of fire flow through my veins.

Now all the males turn to look at me. A few immediately glance back around, knowing they need to do their jobs, but many do the same hair-to-toes once-over. None of them say anything; I assume not wanting to set off Tyree's blazing protective instincts. But the look on their faces was...impressed? Appreciative? Whatever it was, it gives me confidence.

Petra grabs my instruments, and we all surge down the hall. Half the males behind me, half in front.

"Do you want to carry these on stage?" She asks lifting them toward me. "Or should I put them on the table they've set up near your chair?"

I'm on overload; the simple question is too hard to decide.

"I'll put them out there." She glides onstage and leans them against the small table that holds a glass and a pitcher of water.

Tyree edges closer, looking around. Surrounded by so many males, we feel invisible. "Want a quick treatment, *Amara?*"

I nod and furtively touch the hand that's resting at his side. I'm bathed in warmth and serenity.

"You know you'll do well, Grace. We all know how magnificently you play. Want advice?" I nod again. "Look at the back doors. Focus on one of the shining gold knobs. Not the faces, not the people, not whether they appreciate your music or not. Just the knobs. The knobs and your music. Dive into your music, play your program, then stand up and receive your applause. I'll be right here when you're finished."

And that's just what I do. When I'm given my cue, I walk to the oh-my-God golden throne sitting center stage. The applause is thunderous and I know I can't just sit down. I open my arms and raise them, giving the impression I'm receiving their adoration. In reality, I'm focused on a shiny gold knob that seems like a football field away.

As the applause dies down, I take my seat, grab String Thing for my first piece, and dive in. I sink deeper into the music with every lilting note. I soar with the lively compositions and become melancholy with the serious ones. I'm so immersed in the music I realize I'm improvising during one of my favorite songs, *Transformation*, that I composed for Tyree. I have such a deeper connection to him now—new variations of music simply flow from my fingers.

Before I know it, I've come to the end of my program. The hall is still. I don't even hear a cough or the rustling of fancy silk gowns. Nothing. Now I'm even more fearful of tearing my eyes from the shiny gold knob. But as if on cue, the hall erupts in clapping and appreciative shouts. If I thought the applause at the beginning of my program was thunderous, this is louder by tenfold.

I read once that the best sign of recognition after a performance was immediate silence. It signifies the audience was so mesmerized they were completely transported. I think that's what happened. Warmth spreads through my body as I bathe in their approval.

People are stomping their feet. I finally get the nerve to sneak a peek from the golden knob. Most in the audience are Emirusians and look extremely human. Then I see more unusual aliens peppered throughout the house. A shiny silver one that must be from Steele's planet, an amphibious female wearing a bubbler over her mouth and nose to be able to breathe the air on this planet. So many others I can't take it all in.

And then the hall quiets as a tall male on the first balcony rises to his full height and is escorted by the royal guard toward the stage.

Emperor Quirinus. His uniform is the same blood red as the curtains. His shoulders are covered with gold epaulets. There is a huge red gem, large as a drink coaster, hanging around his neck and resting on his chest. Hair, long and midnight black, is pulled into a braid trailing halfway down his back. And he's heading right toward me.

He's smiling. That's a good sign. He looks younger than I'd expected, maybe a few years older than Tyree. For someone ruling an entire planet, he isn't at all what I'd imagined. For starters, he's gorgeous. Straight nose, square jaw, and amethyst eyes. The contrast between those blazing purple eyes and his jet-black hair is startling...and attractive.

Mauritious, the captain of the guard, joins us on stage and makes quiet introductions, the applause still rolling like thunder in the background.

"Lord Quirinus, may I introduce Miss Grace. Miss Grace, Lord Argento Quirinus."

"Call me Arge," the Emperor croons in a deep, melodious voice.

Am I now on a first-name basis with the Emperor of a planet? Really? Just like that?

Mauritious puts his hands up in a motion designed to quiet the crowd and they do, instantly. After all, their Emperor is standing right there.

"Miss Grace, I want to thank you for your brilliant perfor-mance," the Emperor intones in a voice loud enough to be heard throughout the perfect acoustics of the auditorium. "I'm sure everyone in the audience enjoyed your music as much as I did. I'm certain we would all agree you earned the name 'Musician of Angels.'" Oh no, the applause starts up again. I just want to get off this freaking stage before I barf all over his Highness.

Mauritious quiets the crowd again, and the Emperor continues, "As a token of my appreciation...," He lifts the humongous ruby necklace off his neck and places it over my head. My knees start to buckle, not from the weight of the necklace, although it is considerable, but from complete overload. I've reached my limit. Dear Lord, this thing must weigh a pound.

The Emperor is the first to notice that I'm falling in slow motion. He steps closer, grabs me under one arm and pulls me upright.

"Thank you, Your Highness. I'm afraid..."

"Let's get you off this stage," he whispers in my ear, then addresses the crowd, "Thank you all for coming."

Tyree

My chest swelled with pride for Grace. She far exceeded expectations up on that stage. I wonder if she did what I suggested and didn't look at the faces in the crowd. It would be wonderful if she could appreciate the adoration she's receiving from the audience. I hope so—she deserves it. My Gods, her music is amazing. Listening always wrings so many emotions out of me.

I was surprised to see the Emperor approach her on the stage, stunned when he put that expensive, ostentatious gem around her neck, and shocked when her knees began to buckle. I tried to make my way to her side, but without the aid of flight, I could never get there in time.

My jaw set in anger and my eyes narrowed when I saw that pompous *motherdracker* grab her in front of the entire auditorium. Part of my brain understands he was trying to keep her from crashing to the floor. The other part of my brain wants to dismember the bastard one limb at a time.

The front curtain closes, so the audience is hidden from view. The other gladiators and I rush to Grace's side. I ease her into the comfortable chair she performed on. Petra produces a glass of water, and the males form a circle around all of us—backs toward us, faces turned outward.

"I'm fine," Grace sputters as she pushes the water away. Petra's having none of it and keeps urging her to drink.

"I watched you, Grace. You didn't take a sip, not one sip, during the entire two-hour performance. Drink!"

Grace complies, then tries to rise from her chair. I step behind her and gently press her shoulders down before she's six *inces* out of the chair. "Please, my lady, sit. At least for a moment until you're more stable."

I push my calming treatment at her, but I'm not certain she needs it or if she's simply exhausted and dehydrated.

Shadow steps forward and approaches the Emperor. He's taller than the monarch, so he crouches slightly and keeps his eyes obsequiously on the floor. "Your Highness. I know Miss Grace was looking forward to supping with you after the performance, but it appears she will not be up to the task. I apologize for all of the effort you dedicated to what I'm certain would be a most sumptuous meal. Perhaps we could reschedule for another time?"

His eyes remain cast downward; he's still as a statue. Although everything sounds innocuous, every male in the room is on guard, hands surreptitiously on their weapons, waiting to see how the Emperor receives this rebuff.

"Of course. It appears the concert took more out of her than I'd imagined. Do you need help moving her to her rooms?" The Emperor's lips press into a thin line, but his words remain gracious.

"How kind of you to offer. I'm certain we can take it from here." I've got to give Shadow credit; he managed that like a champion.

I sweep Grace into my arms and stalk toward the dressing room. The other males fall in around us, and we're back in our quarters in a moment.

"She didn't eat all day," I bark at no one in particular. "Can we get her some soup, a sandwich and one of those pastries they filled the room with earlier? Didn't we have like a hundred of them? Aren't there any left?"

"I think I ate them all," Dax admits sheepishly. "They were so *dracking* delicious."

I try not to chuckle. Dax is the tallest of us all, pushing seven *fiertos*. He looks as if he could bite someone's jugular for sport. He obviously has a weakness for sweets.

A moment later, it's just Grace and me in her room. She's sitting in a chair and I'm plying her with food.

"I'm not a baby," she protests when I try to feed her soup.

"Well, you didn't exactly use your best judgment by not eating all day. Here." I press half a sandwich into her hand.

She takes a bite, then, "Oh my God. I don't think this is mystery meat. I think this is beef." She pulls the bread off and eats the roast beef with her delicate fingers. A moan escapes her mouth. "Dear Lord, rare roast beef. Best thing I've eaten in months. Don't you dare tell me what this is. I want to go to my deathbed believing this is dead, butchered, harmless cow."

She eats two more sandwiches, passing on the pastries we wheedled out of the Emperor's personal chefs.

"Dax, I think we found you seconds!" I call. He knocks gently, then practically bowls me over to get to the food.

"If you'd call Petra, she can help me out of this dress then I'm going to crawl into bed. So tired."

"I could help..." I whisper, but we both cast our glances at the ceiling, assuming there are eyes and ears attending to our every move.

When I return to the room, Grace is sitting up in bed, looking regal in a white lace sleeping gown provided by the house staff from the costume department.

"You look so sleepy, my lady. I'll lie here by the side of your bed. You go to sleep. The males are taking turns staying awake in the anteroom for your protection. Dax is first. He says his stomach is killing him and he won't be going to sleep soon anyway."

"Tyree, I don't want you..." she frowns at the pallet I'm making on the floor out of extra blankets.

I glance at the ceiling and shrug my shoulders. "I'll be most comfortable on the floor, my lady. I but live to serve." I bow respectfully.

"Tyree, my ever-faithful servant." She smiles.

"I'll be back in a few *minimas*, going to take a quick shower." I haven't had a moment to relieve my aching hard-on all day. *Drackhead* and his two friends are causing considerable pain.

Chapter Eleven

I'm just about asleep when Tyree quietly opens the bath-room door. He has a plush gold towel slung low over his hips. The picture of his burnished skin in the faint light peeking through the crack under the door propels me into full wakefulness.

I've noticed I'll get blind to how handsome he is because I've been around him all day, and then I'll catch a glimpse of him from an odd angle and my breath will catch in my throat from the sheer force of how attractive he is.

My sleepiness slips away, and I swallow hard, aware of sensual warmth flowing through my veins. He stalks over to me with the grace of a big cat. He's so masculine as he leans down and protectively makes sure I'm thoroughly covered.

"Need a treatment?" he whispers.

"Well...yes. But maybe of a different sort." I give him a lazy smile, flirtatious and full of promise. It's an easy thing to do knowing we can't act on our impulses with cameras watching our every move.

We don't want to blow our cover that I'm not really the galaxy's premier musician traveling with a cadre of hard-assed gladiators. It wouldn't be safe for them to know we're just a ragtag bunch of runaway slaves on the lam from the most vicious cartel in the known universe.

"I have an idea," he whispers. "Trust me?"

I nod.

He lies on his pallet, which is right next to my bed. I see him shift under the covers, then throw his towel on the floor. Knowing he's lying inches from me, completely nude makes my stomach tighten in need. My thoughts arrow back to the night we shared a shower and so much more in my bedroom. My clit quivers as I visualize a photo album of pictures from that encounter. I studiously avoid thinking of the terror I experienced when I thought we'd be imprisoned and separated. Nor do I want to think about his sweet proclamation that I'm his truemate—there'll be time to deal with that when we're back on the *Warrior*.

I feel something odd, like a presence in my mind. I pull my thoughts from my pulsing nether regions to my head and pay attention. This is nothing like the calm feeling he pushes at me to reduce my anxiety. This is...fuller, more connected.

Can you hear me, Grace?

I'm startled, and a little afraid. *Yes?*

Sorry I couldn't explain this to you before I began, but there was no opportunity. I have some very...interesting ideas I thought we could explore. You in your bed, me in my pathetic little pallet on the floor. But I have to make certain you're comfortable with this. It's pretty...intimate.

He's in my mind. A frisson of panic bolts up my spine. *Can you read my thoughts?*

I haven't always had this ability. I'm still figuring things out. What I do to calm you, that's basically step one. What I want to do right now is step two. It allows us to talk, for me to hear the thoughts you push at me, but I'm not rummaging around in there. Step three would be what I did with Captain Gren a few times, I read his thoughts. Trust me, it was like bathing in sewage. The sadistic pictures that ran through his mind gave me nightmares. Step four would be what I did to him the day we overthrew the ship. I crawled into his mind and made him do things.

You have to know I would never do that to you, Grace. I wouldn't read your thoughts. I would never force you to do anything or think anything. I respect you too much.

Funny, I believe him. The Tyree I know would never violate my privacy.

Okay. On Earth, we have the concept of safewords. If one person says the word, the other immediately stops what they're doing. I'd be comfortable if we could do that.

Absolutely, Grace. What's your word?

Red.

All right. Are you ready to do this?

Yes. I have no idea what's coming, but I trust Tyree completely, and I'm aroused wondering what he's going to do next.

Take two fingertips and slide them across your lips. Gently, so soft you can barely feel them.

I do this. Instantly my thoughts are completely on this feeling. It's so gentle it tickles, but it ramps up my arousal. I'm fully focused on this sensation.

What are you feeling?

It instantly dawns on me how intimate this is going to be. I'm going to have to share my feelings—not something I'm used to. I want to do this though; I want to share myself with him. I don't want to hold back anymore. In that concert hall, I just did the bravest thing I've ever done in my life. Why not be courageous now?

It tickles in a sensual way. I tell him. It brings my awareness to my lips. Also to other places on my body.

What other places? The tone of his voice in my head commands a response. For some reason, I like this tone.

My clit. This is harder than I thought it would be.

Do it again.

Okay.

Now the slightest bit harder.

Okay.

What do you feel?

Alive. Sensual. Sexual. The beginnings of need.

Need for what?

Need to be kissed by you. Touched by you. I pause a moment, working up my nerve to say the total truth. *Filled by you, Tyree.*

I hear him suck in his breath. *You are the sexiest being in the galaxy, Grace. My cock is hard as stone, just lying by your side. To hear you say that is sweet torture.*

I hear him rustle under his covers, then...*Move your hand slowly down your jaw. Caress your jawline, down the column of your throat, across your collarbones. Do it slowly, pretend it's my hand. It's my fingers exploring you, wanting to learn every hollow, every curve.*

I do this, imagining his fingers traversing my skin in wonder. This causes my mundane body, this skin I've worn for twenty-six years, to be regarded with awe. As if I've only slipped into this physical form for the first time today. For a moment I wonder if this is what it was like for him to wake up a month ago in his current hulking form, wearing a huge, new body.

What do you feel, Grace?

I hear almost a rush in my ears, like a shiver with noise. It makes all my thoughts quiet down—except my focus on this—my body, what we're doing.

Good. You are so good, Grace. You can say "red" at any time. Do you want to go farther?

Yes.

I hear a small sigh drift up from below me.

Take the tip of your tongue and trace the outline of your lips. First the top, then the bottom. He pauses for me to do this. What do you feel?

Shivers. Naughty. Expectant.

Good, Grace. Do you want to be naughty? Do you want what comes next to make you feel like a bad girl?

Do I? Is this a fantasy? Do I want to be naughty with Tyree?

I think I do. I can say red if I don't.

Place your fingers on the back of your neck. Pretend they're mine. Sift them through your hair. Gently. Be patient, like you have all the time in the galaxy. What do you feel?

Tingly. Like every cell above my neckline is more awake than it's ever been. More fully alive.

You are so good to do this. To do just what I say. Do you want to do more of what I say?

I don't need to think. I just answer. *Yes.*

Take your right hand and trail it down from the swell at the side of your breast to the curve of your waist, around your hip to below your knee. Take your time. What do you feel?

Liquid fire. Hot and cold. Shudders and warmth. Every cell is being turned from neutral to fully on—aware.

Do the same thing with your left hand.

I don't know where I get the nerve to tell him how I feel without his question, but I offer, *Every cell is on fire. My... clit is, too. And my core.*

Grace, you are such a good girl. Do you like it when I call you a good girl?

Yes.

Then I want you to be a very good girl and dip both hands below the hem of your gown. With just your index fingers, I want you to lift the hem up. Slowly. Slowly. Let me imagine that white gown edging deliberately up toward your knees, past them, and now, even more slowly up your creamy thighs. Can you hear my heavy breathing, Grace? Do you know how aroused I am just imagining what your hands are doing? Do you want to know that my fist is curled around my cock? It's kicking in my hand just thinking about you. Do you know that?

I can imagine that, Tyree. Your hand tight on your thick cock. Someday I would love to fully taste you there. To suck you all the way into my mouth. I hear his sharp intake of breath and the softest moan.

Did you hear me moan, Grace? I guarantee that in the next hoara I'm going to hear you moan. That's a guarantee. Unless you say the word "red."

My lips are sealed.

Good. Now slip your fingers higher up your thighs to your waist. Imagine my eyes on you. Imagine I'm looking at you right now. I am. I see your lovely pale skin. I see the blond hair at the apex of your thighs. What do you feel?

I'm embarrassed just thinking of it. And aroused. And a little part of me wants to open myself to you and show you all of me. I hear a heavy exhalation from him. I feel powerful knowing I have this effect on you, Tyree.

Do I have an effect on you, Grace?

Yes. I have a need building inside of me.

Good. Tell me about the need.

I first have to pay attention to the feeling. Then I have to determine a way to explain it. *It's tight. My awareness is keenly focused on swirling energy that pools at the tips of my breasts, the top of my cleft, my core. It feels...unfinished. Not quite pain, but not quite pleasure. It's waiting for som ething...to be fulfilled.*

What I just told him was harder than playing up on that stage tonight. I don't know where I found the courage.

Thanks for sharing that with me, Grace. I can't touch you tonight, but I will make sure you are fulfilled. Slip your fingers all the way up, so your gown is resting above your magnificent breasts.

Okay.

Take both hands and cup them below your breasts. Graze your hands from under your breasts to collar bones. Then back down and up again. Slowly.

My mouth is open now. I'm breathing in petite little gasps. My skin is on fire, Tyree. I wish these were your hands. I don't know if I've ever wanted anything more desperately than your hands on me right this minute.

You will, though, Grace. By the end of this night, you'll want many things more desperately than you do right now. Do you doubt that?

No, Tyree. I believe you.

Good girl. Now take the index finger of one hand and place it on the opposite nipple. Draw a line down your breast, through the valley between them and to the other peak. Just the pad of your fingertip. Just the slightest pressure. Back and forth. Until I tell you to stop.

Oh. So good.

Yes. Now use your fingernail. The point of your fingernail from peak to peak. Are your nipples straining to receive the touch?

Yes.

Do they want more?

Yes.

Stop. Just wait.

Oh. It hurts. I hurt with need.

Yes. That's just what I want. I want you to hurt with need. Where does it hurt?

Between my legs.

I would be there right now. My head between your legs if there were no cameras in this room. But there are. I'm going to torture you tonight. Unless you say "red."

My lips are still sealed.

Good girl. Take the thumb and forefinger of each hand and grasp your nipples. Good?

Yesss.

Tell me you're imagining those are my fingers.

Yes.

Pluck the tips. Pluck them and twist them. Just like I did the other night. Just the way you like it.

I let out a tiny sigh.

You're being naughty, Grace. You don't want them to hear you, or do you? Would it make it more arousing to know someone is watching what you're doing to yourself?

No. No. Only you. I wish you were watching.

So do I, Amara. I am watching, in my mind's eye. Lick your fingers and your thumbs and go back to doing what you were doing. Plucking those beautiful pink nubs. Pulling and twisting them. Use one word to tell me how this feels.

Incredible.

Good. Imagine my mouth on you there. Imagine my teeth grazing you. I would start soft and then increase until it was almost too exquisitely hard to bear. Would you like that?

Yes.

Good. Keep touching yourself with your fingers. Raise your heels until they touch your bottom. What are you aware of?

My clit is pulsing. My core is clenching. I'm thinking of your fingers inside me the other night. Your cock inside me. I wish I could feel that again.

Good. I wish I could slip my fingers into your wet warmth. And my cock, Grace. I want my cock buried inside you, joining us together. That will happen again if you want. But not tonight. Now allow your knees to open outward until they touch the bed. I want you to do this slowly. I want you to imagine I'm on my knees in front of you. I'm looking at you. Admiring you. I want you to reveal yourself to me in the slowest tempo possible. Can you do that?

Yes.

I'll describe it. I saw it the other night and the image is branded on my brain. Your folds are like the pink petals of a delicate flower. The bud at the top is juicy and plump. Engorged so that it can garner pleasure. I'm a male now, Grace. I don't like to share. I would like to believe I will be the only male who will ever see that sight. The only male who will ever give you pleasure like that. Tonight I'll watch in my mind's eye as you give yourself that pleasure. Are your knees on the bed yet?

Yes.

Good. Take one or two fingers and dip them in your core—just the pads of your fingers. Tell me what you feel.

Wetness, Tyree. I'm sopping wet. I'm drenched for you. I'm pulsing down there. I can't find any thoughts but these. I can only focus on my body, my skin, my need, and what you're telling me to do.

Good, Grace. Because in a short while, I'm going to tell you to come. And you are going to do exactly that. You are going to come the modicum I tell you and not a moment before. Do you understand?

Yes.

Take those fingers, they should be saturated with your cream, and drag them up through your folds to your sensitive bud. Tell me what you feel.

Shaky. Needy. Desperate.

I'm going to make you feel more desperate, Grace. I'm going to make you so desperate you'll beg for release. Are you willing to follow my instructions? To wait until I allow you to come?

Yes.

Good girl. Take those fingers and slip them down through your folds to where you're flooded with your juices, then slide them up again and circle your bud. Now do it again. Are you good and wet?

Yes.

Do you wish it was my fingers, Grace?

Yes, Tyree. I can imagine it's your fingers.

Do you wish my tongue was swirling around that little pink nub right now?

Yes. Oh my God, yes.

Good. I want you to allow your fingers to move just the way you like. The way that makes your hips thrust and grind. The way that makes you pant and yearn for release. And I don't want you to come. Tell me when you're desperate. More desperate than you've ever felt.

He's quiet. There's no noise in the room. No noise in my head. But I can still feel him here. He's with me—waiting.. .listening. I can feel myself ramping up. Fire is sliding along my veins. My clit is throbbing and needy and yes, desperate, but not more desperate than it's ever been. I tease myself to new heights. I dip my fingers in my core again. I'm saturated with my juices. My need is spiraling higher. I want to make noise, to moan, to grunt, to beg.

I glance down quickly and see that although my hand is circling furiously, the movement can't be seen from above the covers. The eye in the sky could never detect what's going on.

My hand is moving faster, my knees are pressing into the bed as if I'm opening myself to Tyree, even though he's two fucking feet and a million miles away.

Tyree. Now. I'm desperate.

Good girl, Grace. Slow down for a moment. Do it for me.

Oh, don't ask that.

I __am__ asking, Amara. Slow down. Keep touching yourself, but less pressure and slower.

I'm beginning to hate you.

Are you saying "red"?

No!

Are you touching yourself slower and softer?

Yes.

What a good girl you are. I will definitely allow you to come, but not right now. I can hear your breathing slow. Still desperate?

Yes.

More desperate than you've ever been?

No.

Good. Tell me, Grace. When we're off this dracking *planet and we're alone in a bedroom, what are you willing to do to thank me for letting you come?*

Anything.

Get creative, Amara. *Make me an offer.*

Anything you want, Tyree.

Whisper to me, inside your head, Miss Grace. I know you're shy. Keep touching yourself and tell me what you would do for this explosive orgasm I'm going to allow you to have.

I want you to take me, Tyree. Anywhere you want, any way you want. I can't be more specific than that. Please. Please, can I come?

You can touch yourself the way you were before. Harder and faster.

I'm going to die. Can a person die from being too horny? Oh my God. I want to come so badly I feel like I'm going to come apart.

Please, Tyree. Please. Please.

Yes, Grace. I want you to come. Now!

And just like that, as if my body is a puppet that can perform on command I come with an orgasm that feels like rolling thunder. It begins heavily in my pelvis; every muscle contracting at once, allowing instant relief from the buildup of arousal, yet ramping it up even more. I have absolutely no control over the deep moan that explodes out of me. Tyree begins a loud coughing fit. Even in my bliss I know he's covering for me, not wanting our "hosts" to hear the intimate noises of my sexual release.

I continue to ride the waves of my convulsive peaking as he coughs loudly. My thigh muscles are quivering, still spasming. My inner muscles are clenching, wishing they had something to clamp down on. My jaw tightens. My eyes are pressed shut so tightly tears are squeezing from the corners of my eyes. It takes long moments of aftershocks to come down.

Oh my God, Tyree. Oh my God. Thank you.

Thank you, Grace. That felt amazing to me, too. I'll be back in a minima.

I know why he's going to the bathroom. I don't blame him. How could he have lived through that and not want release for himself?

As he rises from his pallet, he tells me, *I'm going to slip out of your thoughts,* Amara. *You go to sleep. I'll see you in the morning. Sleep tight. Know that you are well and truly cared for.*

Tyree

My first thoughts upon awakening are of Grace...and last night. Gods, she is so feminine, so responsive. She was so open to me last night. It felt as though the barriers she always erects disappeared and I slipped behind her defenses for the first time. She's never revealed her true self to me like that before.

I don't care if she's not the truemate I would have found on Larian. She's the mate I want. There will be no other female I could ever desire the way I want her.

After my Transformation, I worried if I'd ever become legitimately masculine, or if I'd forever be in the limbo of confusion about who I truly am. I'm not confused anymore.

I'm male. I may not ever be able to fight in the gladiator ring or master the chainsticks, but what happened between Grace and me last night proved everything I need to know. I want to protect my female, I want to ease her fears, and I want to breach her, enter her, give her ecstasy. I'm all male—and I want to be *her* male.

Drackhead woke before I did. He is hard, insistent, throbbing. Just thinking about her incendiary release makes me want one of my own. Time for another shower, and then I need to find her some food.

Chapter Twelve

GRACE

I wake for the first time in days with no anxiety—zero. Yes, I know I have a performance tonight, and tomorrow. I'll weather it. Everyone loved me last night. My fingers can play my music without direction from me. We'll be off this planet in less than forty-eight hours and I'll never see any of these people again.

And Tyree? I'm not certain I even want to think about what happened last night. But, of course, my mind sprints to a complete, face-reddening rehash of every second. I can't believe I revealed myself to him like that. I let him into my head for God's sake. Not only did I allow him to crawl into my mind, but if that wasn't enough, I told him every thought I had. Every sexy, intimate thought. And every feeling—every horny feeling. I described how he made me feel. Oh my God, I practically promised to be his sex slave when we got back to the ship. My ears are burning in embarrassment.

At the time, it was exciting and sensual and like agreeing to a sexy dare. Now, this morning, I feel like I did something while I was drunk that I'm regretting the day after. If I was a sorority girl, I would do the walk of shame out of the frat house and hope I never ran into the guy on campus. But Tyree is my personal bodyguard! He's not going to leave my side for the next two days. And then we'll be back onboard the *Warrior* along with twenty other souls. How am I supposed to avoid him?

I hear a muffled grunt from the bathroom, then a flush, then the shower running. The man is one big walking hormone. And it's all directed at me. This thought pricks my nipples, now standing in tight points under my gown. The same gown I pulled up my body as if I was exposing myself to him last night.

"Stop it, Grace!" I order myself. I don't even care if whoever is monitoring me thinks I'm crazy. Perhaps I am.

I get up, pull a blanket around me, and march down the hall in search of an empty bathroom. The suite is bustling with activity. Half the males are already dressed in their uniforms, the others seem to all be noisily showering in every available bathroom. I skulk back to my room. I'll have to deal with Tyree sooner than I'd like.

When I approach, Petra's standing at my door, about to knock. "Oh, Grace. Dax and Theos went back to the ship and grabbed us all some clothes since we hadn't planned on sleeping here. Clean panties!" She holds a pair aloft and waves them like a flag, "And a few of your dresses, as well as a large t-shirt to sleep in. I hope you don't mind that he pawed through your stuff to find this."

"Great!" I try to sound cheerful. "I was wondering what I was going to wear today."

Luckily, Tyree is dressed when I crack the door to our room.

"Morning," I say, avoiding his eyes as I skirt around him, enter the bathroom, and close the door behind me. I'm sure that was as obvious as a slap in the face. I immediately turn on the water to drown out any questions he may be lobbing at me through the door, although I know I'll have to face him at some point.

In less than ten minutes, I've showered, dragged a comb through my hair, and pulled on underwear and a dress. Moment of truth. When I open the door, though, he's gone.

Why are my lips pressed into a thin line of dejection when I realize he's not here?

Obviously, I don't know what I want. Half of me wants to avoid him for the rest of my life, the other half doesn't want to be separated from him for more than a minute. Perhaps insanity runs in my family. Maybe I'm as unbalanced as my mother.

I know something's wrong as soon as I open the door to our hallway. It's quiet. Like eerily quiet. Gladiators are not quiet people. They're big and loud and uninhibited—even when they're wearing clothes, and that isn't all the time. They laugh and joke and make fun of each other, that is when they're not farting or arm wrestling or arguing over who gets the last pastry—which is always Dax by the way.

I walk into the sitting room, where everyone is quietly gathered, and it's like that old game of telephone where one person whispers in another's ear and the secret is passed around. In this version, as each person receives the information their face becomes pinched, their eyes downcast, their whole expression somber.

By the looks of it, Tyree has already heard the secret. When he sees me, his eyes dance from mine.

I'm sure you're wondering what's going on, his thoughts flash into my mind. *Dax and Theos went back to the ship and came back with some disturbing news. Callista has been monitoring deep space comms and has some serious concerns. We're all but certain that the Bird of Prey II, one of MarZan's swiftest vessels, is on its way here. They've tracked our ship. Zar's thought is to leave atmo and lead them on a chase. Luckily our hyperdrive was repaired yesterday.*

Okay. I respond. *I'll grab my things. I'm certain the Emperor isn't going to like this, but we've got a fast ship and can be far away from this planet before they know we're gone.*

We don't need another enemy, Grace. His brow furrows in determination. *MarZan knows every gladiator on the ship.*

*They were idented and well documented. They would never suspect me, I was three-*fiertos *tall. The women's info never left the ship. I'm convinced they won't be looking for either of us. You and I will be safer here on Emirus.*

Separate from everyone? My eyes are wide in panic. These people have become my family. I feel safe on the ship. If we separate, I won't have all my friends.

They'll come back to get us, Grace. The crew will just have outrun MarZan and come back to pick us up when it's safe. That way you won't incur Emperor Quirinus' wrath. I don't want to be on his bad side. He doesn't look like the forgiving type.

So, Tyree, everyone would take off and leave us here? Just like that? What about our safety?

The Emperor has been generous with his personal guards. We don't have to even leave our quarters. We'll just sit tight here and await pickup.

I hate to express my next fear, but it has to be communicated, *What if...what if they never come to pick us up? What if the cartel...?"*

We've discussed that possibility. This is a civilized planet. You have your music, you'll always be able to earn credits—you can live here comfortably. You'll have me as your bodyguard. People have been stranded with far fewer resources.

I care for everyone on board, even Shadow. I don't want to contemplate losing them. They're my family more than my mother ever was. It strikes me with sudden force that I have a family now. And I might lose them. I swallow several times in rapid succession, trying not to release the tears threatening to spill from my eyes.

We're waiting for a signal from Zar. Tyree continues. *The ship is still monitoring comms. If our suspicions are confirmed, the males and Petra will be gone within* mini-mas—*she refuses to leave her male. Shadow will give me his wrist comm so they can keep in touch with me regarding retrieval. We'll tell Emperor Quirinus the captain's mother is ill and they have to fly through a hazardous quadrant to get to his home planet. We'll tell him how safe we feel here, and that we'll stay until our comrades return.*

He smiles to reassure me, but he's a terrible liar. Plans this hasty rarely work.

MY HAND IS SHAKING as I try to apply makeup as skillfully as Petra did last night. We received word that she and the gladiators needed to run. Petra grabbed my green dress, Dax threw about a hundred pastries in a pillowcase, and they were on the *Warrior* by two in the afternoon.

This dress is so heavy and hard to maneuver, it took tremendous effort to struggle into it without assistance. Of course, Tyree would be all too happy to help, but that would tip off the sneaky, watchful eyes. I'm wearing the red dress tonight; my breasts are crammed into the bodice and artfully hidden by lace. I'm wearing the huge, heavy, red gem necklace the Emperor gave me yesterday. It's far too ostentatious for my taste, but looks great with the dress and will express my gratitude for the gift.

Without Petra, my hair isn't nearly as skillfully arranged as it was last night. Yesterday my thin blond hair had been coaxed into a chic chignon. Today I've pulled it back into an easy ponytail at the nape of my neck. It will have to do.

But the makeup, well, that's another story. My mom used to go "out on the town" as she put it, which meant fire engine red lipstick, way too much blush, and her boobs on display. She usually did this when she had no boyfriend and needed drugs. As I grew older, I got a very clear idea of what else this entailed.

Because of this, I never went through the preteen phase of playing with my mom's makeup. I've never worn anything with more color than cherry ChapStick. I know I'll look washed out from the audience if I don't have on some fairly heavy cosmetics, but I have no idea how to accomplish this. I've put products on and washed them off four times now, and my face hurts from all the scrubbing.

Tyree knocks on the door. "Grace. I contacted the ladies from the dress shop. They agreed to give you a hand. I knew you needed help."

Help? From the neon ladies? Um, what could they possibly offer me? I'm desperate and let them in.

"I showed them some pictures I took on my wrist comm last night. They say they can help you with that look," he assures me.

"No neon? I don't want to look like a prostitute."

"They assure me they understand."

Thirty minutes later I'm nodding my head in approval at my reflection. The eye shadow is a little more dramatic than I'd like, but it's artfully applied and coordinates with the red of the dress.

I realize I've been so consumed with hair and makeup that I've had little chance to meltdown over the elephant in the room, or should I say elephants? The fact that I'll be playing in front of thousands of people in under an hour, my friends on the *Warrior* are probably in another sector by now, and I'll be dining with the Emperor of the planet after my performance. Not to mention the awkward strain between Tyree and me.

He pays the ladies for their time with the card Shadow gave him before he left. As soon as they leave, he sits me down, stands behind me and gives me a chaste neck rub the cameras can't miss. This gives him the opportunity to give me a treatment that allows me to take full, deep breaths.

You'll do fine, Amara. *The same as last night, only better—and easier. Did staring at the doorknob help?*

Yes, I should have told you. It worked great.

So do that, Grace. Focus on that and let your fingers fly. Your program will be over before you know it.

And that's exactly what happens. I forget the *Battle-Scarred Warrior*. I don't pay attention to the fact Emperor Quirinus has chosen to attend two performances in two days. I don't notice the thousands of eyes watching my every move. I just allow my fingers to fly, as Tyree suggested. The program is over in what seems like a few minutes.

Tyree

Grace's performance was even more accomplished and well-received than it was last night. I'm so proud of her.

Shadow had spoken with Mauritious about our departure before the gladiators left the planet. He didn't think there was any suspicion that something was amiss. By the look of things, I don't think the Emperor gave it another thought. No, he was too *dracking* busy figuring out a way to get Grace alone in his private, concert-hall suite.

I want to kill him. My hands are fisted at my sides and I hear blood pounding in my ears. He told Grace she'd be safe with him and his guards. He urged me to take a "well-deserved night off." He caught me alone in the hallway and pointed out a lovely young female, her breasts exposed above a fancy gown, her nipples rouged, evidently to appeal to a male's baser instincts.

"Why don't you leave Grace here with me? She'll be protected as heavily as if she was in the bosom of her own family. See that beautiful female over there? The four-armed Mordite with the lush mouth and luscious breasts? She is well trained. She's so desirous to please whatever male I suggest, she doesn't need to wear a pain/kill collar. She would be eager to service you tonight. All night long." He leers at me lasciviously.

"She was trained in the Moruvian Butterfly Technique, young man. The Moruvian Butterfly Technique," he repeats as he flicks his thick crimson tongue quickly in and out of his lips. "It is said there is nothing more arousing in all the galaxy. Leave Grace with me. Go have fun."

"I've been charged by her father to protect her since she was a schoolgirl, your Highness. Besides, he would have my head and the heads of my parents if I was derelict in my duties." I glance at the female and now understand the dead look in her eyes. "The Moruvian Butterfly Technique. I've heard about it since my teens. Many said it was simply legend. I'm certain it would be wonderful. You're generous to make such an offer. I'm sorry I have to decline."

In the Emperor's private suite I move to Grace's side to pull out the chair for her at the table for two that has been sumptuously set. I position myself in the corner so I can watch the two of them.

There are no less than eight of the Emperor's personal guards in this room. If he gave the signal, my head would be separated from my neck before I could draw my gun. So be it. I'll keep playing this game of courtly manners. I'll protect Grace with my last breath.

Out of all the males on the ship, I am least equipped to actually protect my *Amara*. I'm clumsy with the chainsticks lodged in a holster at the small of my back. I'm slow to draw my gun. I've only sparred in hand-to-hand combat a handful of times. I should have demanded one of the other males stay to safeguard Grace. I was too possessive to properly assess what would have been best for her security.

Now look at her. She seems to be enamored of this male. I can see his appeal. He's so wealthy and powerful—that alone would make any female's heart flutter. But I have to admit, his crimson lips and dark features are handsome in a cruel way. Cruel, yes that's the word I've been searching for. It was there all along, but most apparent when he was speaking of the Mordite female. This male likes his power.

I attempt to stay out of the way. I don't show any attachment to Grace other than that she is my charge. I keep my features schooled in a soldier's attentive repose. It wouldn't do any good for my face to expose my desire to rip his jugular out of his throat.

He reaches across the table to feed Grace a piece of *breen* he has declared "impeccably cooked." Is she simpering? Enjoying his attention? Really? Perhaps my psychic powers extend to being able to set this room ablaze and kill us all.

But no, I stand here, the perfect picture of the lone gladiator. Protector and servant. The only thing that keeps me from embarking on a killing rampage is the memory of Grace under her covers last night. Mine. She's mine, even if right now at this moment she's laughing at his lame jokes.

I'm fully aware of what is currently going on in this room, but I'm nursing the memory of Grace's wild orgasm last night. Although this dinner is interminable, it will be over soon. Grace will be with me tonight. Even though I'll be sleeping on the floor, we'll be in the same room. He will never have her.

There's something about the look that just slashed across his face. It's only apparent for a moment. I don't think Grace caught it. Her facial muscles don't tighten, her shoulders don't stiffen. But I can't shake my concern. The demeaning way he talked about the Mordite female. The casual way he referenced her slave collar. He was so proud she was his possession and so well trained she would do his bidding without needing punishment. The way he offered her to me like he offered Grace a piece of *breen*.

The thought at first insinuates itself into my brain—I push it away. But the idea won't let go—I should glimpse his thoughts. At first, I think it's an idea from *Drackhead*. *Drackhead's* ideas are seldom worth acting upon. But this thought has more merit than that. What happened with Grace and me last night leaves no doubt I can accomplish it. Even though he's a different species, I know I can climb into his mind.

The more I contemplate it, the deeper the thought burrows into my brain. A few moments later, I quit debating with myself—I know I'm going to do it. And a *modicum* after that I school my features into easygoing indifference, lock my hands behind my back in a placid "at ease" position, and let the fingers of my mind reach gently into his.

Last night with Grace, I knocked at the door of her mind. Now, though, the tendrils of my mind slip under the doorway of his like wisps of smoke. My entry is undetected. He's still blustering at Grace, bragging about battles of bygone *annums* as the general of his father's troops. I begin pillaging through his thoughts, looking for the doorways to his hidden memory closets.

And then I find it. The secret closet at the back of his mind. When I open it, I realize that what I see makes the raw sewage I encountered in Captain Gren's mind seem like a clear forest stream.

I toggle back to this room, making certain my features are set like stone. I don't want to give anything away. Grace is safe. Neither the Emperor nor any of his guards are alerted to any change in me. Then I return to rummage through the ruler's secret closet.

I see him as a little boy, hitting his personal servant, a grown male, over and over with a cane. The cane whistling, the male wailing in pain, his blood dripping from dozens of slices decorating his back and thighs. For a moment I'm privy to the absolute jubilation the young Emperor felt wielding this amount of power.

The next memory I open is the Emperor...*drack*, I don't want to watch. What was seen cannot be unseen. I already saw his penis enter his female pet. I don't know what type of animal it is. It reminds me a bit of my four-legged Druselda back home. She was my constant companion—so loyal. I have to shut the door on this heinous memory without watching it to the end. This was just too unsettling. Nausea rises from my stomach. I saw more than enough.

Again I bring my attention back to scan this room. I want to make sure no tears are leaking out of my eyes. Perhaps it's because I lived so many *annums* as a slave. Or maybe I just have innate compassion. Watching this is like having a hand squeezing my heart.

But I have to open some other doors. Perhaps those were aberrations of a young male with too much time and not enough parental attention. I slip back into his mind and already know which door I need to open. It's well worn. I have a hunch it's his favorite.

This isn't from his childhood or adolescence. It looks like it could have happened yesterday. It's him and a young female. She could be a Morganian like Shadow, but for some reason, I wonder if she's human. Her skin is ruddy amber; she's lovely—tall and delicate. She's crying and shaking her head. Her body is nude and quaking so vigorously it's a wonder she can stand.

The bedroom is huge and so well-appointed it has to be his. It's done up in blood red and gold. Everything is sumptuous and expensive. But that's not what keeps my attention. He's ordering her around. He doesn't raise his voice. I doubt he needs to. She wears a pain/kill slave collar, he wears the wrist controller. She's crying, begging. He just keeps calmly repeating his commands. He orders her to her knees. He orders her to suck his cock. He orders her to do other odious things.

Then I realize there's another soul in the room. Oh, my Gods, this male looks like pictures from the scriptures my parents read to me as a child. The book called him *Suratan*. He was pure evil. And that is what this man looks like. His face is red, white, and black, with savage markings—almost like a skull. He is so fearsome-looking, you'd shoot without asking questions if you encountered him in a back alley.

My blood chills in my veins. I shift back to the present, once again ensuring that my face is emotionless. Grace and the Emperor are on the dessert course. She's cooing and praising the delicacy of the dish he's pressing into her mouth with his fork. My mind flashes a picture of me squeezing his throat so hard his eyes pop out of his skull. I breathe in and out at a slow pace.

This male and his minions are far more dangerous than I'd ever imagined. I have to keep my wits about me. I can't give anything away. Grace isn't in any immediate danger. I need to go back inside that infested pool of waste one more time. I have to see what the Emperor and *Suratan* do to that poor young female.

"Come here, Devolose," the Emperor orders. The *Suratan's* lips are pressed in a flat line. He looks calm and impassive. He doesn't look horrified. He steps forward upon command and bows his head, ready to do the Emperor's bidding.

"Slap Tawny's face!"

Devolose does as he's told immediately and without question.

"Harder!" Devolose slaps her so hard her head swivels on her neck, then ricochets back past the midline of her body.

"Yes!" I can feel the Emperor's glee, as well as his arousal. "Again!" This goes on for agonizing moments. Perhaps out of necessity I discover the mechanism to watch these vids in fast fashion.

Quirinus climbs upon his bed, lies back, and pulls his turgid cock from his trousers. He fondles it slowly, like a male who wants to prolong his pleasure.

"Slap her breasts," he demands. Then, of course, "Harder!"

I clamp my teeth together. I've seen enough. These memories are horrifying, sadistic and recent. I simply can't force myself to watch one more moment.

Just when I think I can leave these scenes, I see another doorway. It also looks well-worn. I know I have to open this door, too. Now that I know how to fast forward, I can handle whatever I find. At least I hope so.

I see a dungeon. It looks old, dark and damp with water dripping from the ceiling. The female is in a cell; the *Suratan* is with her. Perhaps he's some type of android or cyborg? Certainly, no living sentient being could be so impassive, so uncaring.

The Emperor is on his sumptuous bed, fondling his cock much more aggressively and enjoyably than before. He's watching the scene on a screen and giving orders to the Suratan via a comm unit. Somehow I have clarity that this is a frequent pastime for the monarch. He does it often, enjoys it.

The female is locked in his dungeon. She looks worse in this picture. There are bruises in various stages of healing all over her nude body.

One more thing. This will be more dangerous. I have to leave the attic of this maniac's mind and sneak into his current thoughts. I need to find out where this dungeon is, and how to get there. The attic was far away from his current awareness. But this information is right there in his conscious mind. If he feels me riffling through his thoughts I won't be safe. Grace won't be either.

I know the dessert course is over and I'll need to come back to full alertness soon. I ask myself what Grace would want, and I know the answer before I even ask it. She would never allow me to leave that female in the dungeon. I need to know where it is. Later I'll have to figure out how to help Tawny escape. How to kill the *Suratan* and the Emperor? That will have to wait until another day.

Miraculously, the Emperor doesn't feel me searching his mind for the directions to the dungeon. I discover every step—it isn't far.

"Oh, Arge. Thank you for your kind invitation. Whoever would have imagined that I would be invited to inspect the private living quarters of the Emperor of Emirus?" Grace is fawning. Is she enamored? Has he deluded her?

"It is so hospitable of you, but these performances fatigue me so greatly. I'll be useless tomorrow if I don't go to sleep shortly. Thank you again for your generous offer. You've been nothing but kind. This food has been the most delicious I've ever tasted. Seriously. My trip to Emirus will remain in my memories forever. Thanks also for allowing me to pack a portion to give my servant when we're back in my quarters." She lifts the little package that's been wrapped by his staff as if it contained diamonds.

"Tyree, would you escort me back to my room? Thanks again, Argento." She curtsies as if she was born for a life like this. She said her existence on Earth was a struggle. Does the Emperor fulfill her dreams? Did she have fantasies of growing up and living in a palace decorated with gold and gems? My nostrils flare and my hands twitch in envy. Envy at an unspeakable monster, I remind myself.

She bestows a warm, wide smile on him, and I wonder if she's smitten. His veneer is so gracious, so generous, so handsome.

I bend slightly at the waist and gesture for her to precede me out the door. We walk from his huge suite on the first-floor balcony to the stage and then through the maze of hallways to our quarters. Three of the Emperor's guards follow us. If he were to simply give the word, those guards would be our captors, perhaps our tormentors, rather than our protectors.

Grace's safety is so precarious. How can I defend her? One thing I do know. I can't let her know what I just saw in his mind. She would never be able to perform her last concert tomorrow if she knew. I want to rescue the enslaved female. But even more than that, I must keep Grace safe. My Grace.

I'm not much for praying, but I pray with all my heart that Zar and Axxios find a way to outwit and outrun the cartel. I picture them swooping in as Grace takes her final curtain call tomorrow and snatching us off this *dracking* planet.

"WHAT A CHARMING MAN," she sighs after we've both showered and are lying down.

"Indeed," I reply, my tone dripping with sarcasm.

"You didn't eat any of the doggy bag I brought you."

"If the translator is correct, on my planet we do not eat that type of animal, it is considered a house pet."

She laughs, then explains the term.

"Thanks, but I've lost my appetite."

"Seriously the best food I've eaten in my entire life, Tyree. I felt guilty, eating it in front of you and not being able to share. Sure you don't want some now?"

"No appetite," my tone is sour.

"Don't you think the Emperor is handsome?"

What is that inflection in her voice? Is she baiting me? Why?

"And charming. Don't you think he's the most charming fellow?"

My hands ball to fists at my sides. I don't believe I've ever been irritated with Grace before, but my anger gathers so fast my temples throb and my jaw clenches.

"Did it seem to you like he was interested in me, Tyree? Do you think he might have a little crush? Did you know he's not married? Imagine that, a man of his good looks and muscular stature. I was thinking—"

I can't control myself any longer. I roar into her head like the fire stallions from Luxon IV. *Grace!* I scream at her, my anger flaring.

Dear Lord, Tyree. Did you need a written invitation to come talk to me in my head? My next move was to give voice to a sexual fantasy about that horrid male.

Horrid? I slow my breathing and unclench my fists.

Yes, horrid. I've never encountered a male, or female for that matter, so enamored of their own voice. The food was delicious, but the dinner was endless. I could barely wait to come back to our room and giggle with you about what an ass he is. You do think he's an ass, don't you?

Okay, my breathing is almost back to normal, but now I have to figure out how to laugh and joke with her and not let her know exactly how black that male's soul is. I'm assuming he'll be at tomorrow's performance as well. If she knew half of what I know, she'd never be able to tolerate being in the same room with him.

Total ass, I agree. Galaxy's biggest ass.

I got a pervy vibe from him, too. But let's change the subject. I wish we could snuggle in this bed. Although, after what happened last night maybe that's not a good idea. I miss those nights before your Transformation when we'd laugh and have fun watching vids in bed.

We could do that again, Grace. It's just that now we have other things we can do in bed when we're bored. More choices than vids...

Are you leering at me, Tyree? I wish I could see your handsome face. It's kind of interesting not being able to touch. Maybe tonight I could be the one to tell you what to do under your covers.

Mighty bold, Miss Grace. Some night I would like that, too. In fact, I'm moving that very thing to the top of my fantasy list.

Ohhh, very interesting. What's right below that?

I'm at a choice point here, keep up this sexual banter and tease poor *Drackhead* to the point of a trip or two or three to the bathroom, or shut things down right now.

We've got a long day ahead of us tomorrow, and your dracking dinner took hoaras. We should probably save our little games for another time.

You're right. One more day on this crappy planet. One more exhausting performance. Do you think the Sweet Del...The Warrior *will be here tomorrow? I don't even want to think that it might not...Nope not going there.*

Absolutely. Tomorrow. I try to reassure her, even though it might not be true. For all I know everyone on board could be dead right now. We've got good males and females on that ship. I can't allow my mind to think such things. *It will probably touch down before the end of your performance. We'll grab those beautiful gowns of yours and make a run for the ship.*

Do you really think I need those gowns? I'll probably never perform again.

You asked what the next fantasy on my list was? It involves those dresses.

Mmmm, tell me.

Nope, I'll show you. We'll be back on board the ship. In our room. I keep the thought to myself: Because you're mine. We'll sleep in the same room. We'll be truemates.

I turn over to go to sleep then freeze almost as if I'm paralyzed. A thought has been nagging at the back of my mind since that noxious excursion into the Emperor's mind, but I couldn't place it. Now it's like all the little hints are tumbling into place, and it's chilling me to my marrow.

When I was rummaging through that madman's mind something seemed out of place. There was something about the cell next to Tawny's. His thoughts flicked there several times. But the cell was empty.

Maybe he used to have a captive in there and was still thinking about her, but I didn't get any images of that. My heart almost stops beating when I realize I found pictures of Grace in his mind. I was paging through his images so quickly, trying to see the broad view, I let the tiny fragments escape into the river of his thoughts.

But now that I replay what I saw and slow the river down, I see there were two distinct times he pictured my *Amara*. As I stop the vid from running and look closely, I see the pictures aren't of Grace in a green or red dress, but of her nude.

There is a strong hand squeezing my heart. My mouth is parched. I've never felt this level of fear before—even when I was seven and kidnapped by aliens.

The Emperor is a madman, and he wants my *Amara* in a cell. In his dungeon. Next to poor Tawny who he's nearly abused to death.

Almost worse than this is the fact that I'm alone on this planet. I'm less than one lunar cycle post Transformation with no comrades, only one gun, and a pitiful set of chainsticks I don't have the skill to use properly. There's a good chance everyone on the *Warrior* is dead. I can't expect rescue. How can I protect my Grace?

I could be wrong. We could be safe. But we're not. *She's* not. This I know for certain. The one thing in this life I believe I'm meant for is to protect her—and I don't know how.

My mind is racing like the fastest computer, but I can't see any way to keep her safe. I'll try to be clever, to use my abilities, but Quirinus is the most powerful male on the entire planet.

I consider telling Grace, but there's nothing she can do. It will just make her more anxious and miserable. If she plays badly tomorrow God knows what will happen to her.

Then the thought pierces into my brain. If things go badly tomorrow, I want her to know how well and truly I love her. I have to tell her again that I consider her my truemate. Perhaps it's something she can hold onto, to give her strength.

Grace

Grace. Grace, are you still awake?

Mmm-hmm. I was almost asleep. Tyree's voice inside my head sounds different, urgent.

I know the timing is odd, but I wanted to speak to you about something important.

Sure, Tyree. I love talking to you. What's bothering you?

Nothing's bothering me, Amara. *I just think you should know...*

It's like he ran out of gas. The mindlink is severed for a minute, then reconnects.

I told you the other day when we thought we were going to be killed or separated by the Federation, that you're my truemate. I haven't mentioned it since—you've been so pre-occupied with your performance, but I just feel compelled...

He sounds so serious. I'm now fully awake.

I just need to tell you I've known you're my truemate since before our revolution. I want you to know how important you are to me. I realize I've frightened you with talk of truemates. You've avoided it since my poorly-timed disclosure. I won't discuss it again unless you bring it up. But perhaps...there might be a moment when it will be important for you to know...to hold onto the fact that I love you with all my heart, as deeply as a male can love a female.

Tyree, I—

Larian truemates share love, and so much more. I will do anything and everything in my power to make you happy, to provide for you and protect you. I would die for you, Grace.

I stop a moment to consult my heart, which is squeezed in the tightest clench, as I bask in the words this male just said to me. *Tyree, I don't know what to say. That's certainly the sweetest, most impassioned thing anyone has ever said to me.*

I never knew my father. My mom neglected me and allowed others to abuse me, and here the galaxy's sweetest male just declared his undying love for me. A normal person would be swooning, and groveling, and kissing the ground the Larian walks on. But me, abnormal as I am, I'm figuring out how to tell him I'm not interested.

Did I never have that talk with him? The one I should have had about not getting too close? The one where I tell him I can't rely on anyone because I discovered early and often that no one is reliable?

I should explain to him I don't know how to trust. And I should tell him I'm afraid to be dependent on anyone, even him.

My head is spinning when I realize he's silently waiting for a response. He's the nicest male I've ever known—human or otherwise. How do I tell him he should find another truemate, someone who can open her heart fully to him? Someone who isn't neurotic and phobic and as fucked up as I am.

Grace, I can tell by your silence that my words weren't what you wanted to hear. I shouldn't have said them. I'll never bring them up again, it was presumptuous of me to divulge them. You don't have to respond. When we wake up tomorrow let's pretend I didn't say those things. Just go to sleep.

*Tyree, I'm sorry. I care for you, I do. You don't understand what you're asking. I'm messed up, I—*I realize he severed the connection and hasn't heard a word I've said.

Chapter Thirteen

GRACE

This day has been difficult, although Tyree's been the perfect gentleman. I certainly would be a bit more pissy if someone just broke my heart. He's been super protective all day, doesn't want to let me out of his sight. I practically had to physically kick him out of the bathroom when I took a shower. He ordered me to leave the door open a crack, and it wasn't sexual—he was serious. I know he's worried about the crew of the *Warrior*. I am, too. But it seems to be more than that.

He's got a wrist comm connected to the ship, but it won't work until the vessel hits atmo on Emirus.

I don't want to think about my friends on the ship, I don't want to think about the creepy Emperor, I don't want to think about tonight's performance, and I definitely don't want to think about what's going on between Tyree and me.

I know he's a special male. Any woman would be lucky to be with him. He's smart and funny and we always have a great time together. Our sexual chemistry is off the charts. Almost everyone on the ship is coupled up in one way or another. It would be easy to just let the truemates thing happen, whatever that entails.

I've decided sex is pretty terrific, and I don't need to run from that anymore. I'm human. I have needs. I can't think of anyone I'd rather share my body with than him. But more than that? Give my heart to someone? Be desperate and clingy and codependent on a man? Give up huge gobs of myself just to have someone to have sex with or protect me or 'take care' of me? No thank you.

And unfortunately, Tyree wants that. He wants to share a room and be mates like Shadow and Petra, or Zar and Anya. I need to be my own person—to find myself and quit hiding from people. And I need to learn to do that as a single person. Not a couple.

Things have been so tense today—we've barely talked. I should have taken the opportunity to explain myself, but when I practice my speech in my mind it just sounds lame.

Finally, it's time to get ready for my performance. Tonight's the white dress. I saved this for last. It's the most formal and signifies I'm done with this terrible obligation.

I watched the neon ladies very carefully yesterday and I think I can do a serviceable job on my hair and makeup. I'm beyond ready for this day to be over.

THE CONCERT EXCEEDED EXPECTATIONS. I'm receiving a standing ovation and the crowd is roaring its appreciation. Since this is my last performance, I take this opportunity to tear my eyes off the golden doorknob at the back of the hall. There are a lot of Emirusians here, but also a smattering of other races from all over the galaxy.

Now that I pay attention, I see that neon wigs seem to be all the rage for many of the women—and some of the men. I always wondered how people with four arms would manage, but by the looks of them clapping, it works just fine. I don't focus on everyone's differences, I bathe in the fact that their faces all seem to be beaming at me. They truly enjoyed my music tonight, and that makes me feel awesome.

I'm studiously avoiding turning my head to my left, where the Emperor's suite is. I know he's here because he asked me to join him for dinner again tonight. As terrific as the food tasted last night, I don't want anything more to do with him. He had a creepy vibe I'd like to avoid. I try to focus on the applause and not the worries nagging at the back of my mind. I'm terrified that all my friends are dead and no one is coming to take me off this planet. And my heart is breaking for Tyree because by the look on his face, his heart is breaking for me.

Damn, here comes the Emperor, with his contingent of eight guards. Tyree steps out on stage as well, looking strong and handsome in his gladiator uniform—all that burnished skin, all those rippling muscles. He comes to my side and stands, making his protective presence known. The Emperor doesn't even give him a second glance.

The auditorium quiets and Emperor Quirinus announces, "I want to thank you all for attending. I can see we all appreciated Miss Grace's entrancing music tonight. She truly is the Musician of Angels. Perhaps I can convince her to stay right here on Emirus so she can entertain us on a regular basis?"

The crowd erupts in thunderous applause. At first, it seems like an innocent statement, but the way the Emperor's brow furrows, as well as his odd smile, make me wonder if there's a meaning I don't quite understand.

He leans low and whispers in my ear as the audience files out, "Please join me for a bite to eat, Miss Grace."

I nibble my bottom lip, trying to think of a nice way to bow out.

"Your bodyguard is welcome as well. I'm sure you're hungry after that enchanting performance."

"I'm so tired, your Highness. Your offer is so gracious, but..."

"I won't take no for an answer." He smiles, but it comes off as more of a leer.

With that, he gently takes my elbow and pulls me toward his suite. I glance over my shoulder and look at Tyree, hoping my expression conveys the fact that I'm not happy about this. We're totally outnumbered here. I'll have a quick bite and then beg off. Tyree's face looks more like an angry plastic mask than his actual skin. His muscles are tight and his eyes are sending me a message I can't quite read.

"You certainly can be persuasive," I tell the Emperor when we're sitting at a table that is groaning with food in his luxurious suite. "Our ship is coming for us shortly. I'll have to make this quick. I need to get back to my room to pack."

"You've received word from your ship? Your captain's mother's health has improved?" he asks casually as he takes a dainty bite.

"Well," I shrug, "the plan was for them to pick us up tonight after my last performance, no matter her health. He knew his visit wouldn't be a long one."

I'm hating this conversation. I just want to hurry to my room and slip out of this uncomfortable dress.

The Emperor gives a slight nod to Mauritious, and his men move lightning-quick. One guard stands on either side of me, and six surround Tyree, knives pointing at his throat before he can move. Tyree's gun is wrestled from his hand before my mind fully grasps what just happened.

"Let's quit this charade, shall we?" the Emperor says, his tone sharp, his lips curled in derision. "I was aware of exactly who you are within an *hoara* of your arrival on this planet, *my* planet. You males are escaped gladiators from the *Warbird One*, a MarZan cartel ship. I assume you, *Miss* Grace, are one of the Earth females the ship was reported to be carrying. A breeder, I'm told."

I'm trying not to freak out, but I'm certain my trembling chin and flaring nostrils reveal my burgeoning terror.

"Did you not think I would thoroughly investigate every living being who sets foot on my planet? Who do you think told the cartel of your presence here? The fact that your comrades took off and left you was a nice turn of events. I received a hefty reward from the syndicate, as well as the spoils of war my dear...which is you." His polite facade is long forgotten. His face is angry, lips pulled back into a snarl.

"You bastard. You can't do this. You don't know who she is. She has family on Morgana, her father is a prominent businessman. I've been her slave since birth." Tyree tries to break free from the six guards surrounding him, but his effort only results in a nick on his throat from Mauritious' long, sharp knife.

"Shut. Up," the Emperor spits. "I've contacted the authorities on Morgana. She has no wealthy father there. You two are on the run from the cartel. They're going to decimate your little ship, kill all your friends, and I..." He reaches across the table and grabs my throat. "Will take possession..." He squeezes harder in tiny increments until I'm gasping for breath. My fingers clawing at his hands can't pry him off me. "Of the two of you."

He turns to face Tyree, his grip on my throat so tight I'm seeing stars and getting lightheaded. "You'll be quickly dispatched, well...not *too* quickly. The longer it takes, the more amusing it will be to watch. She...," he releases me and I breathe in deep gasps of air. My throat is burning, my eyes are tearing, and my head is spinning with this latest turn of events. "She will be the newest addition to a small but fascinating collection I keep for my personal amusement."

Tyree

I quit struggling. I need every ounce of my energy to focus on getting us out of here, or at least getting Grace out of here; I consider myself expendable. I need to think this through. The bastard has us captured. He has an unlimited supply of armed guards at his disposal. I'm a single male with marginal fighting skills and no gun. I can't count on being rescued. From what the Emperor says, MarZan knew exactly who we were and exactly where to find us. I can only believe my friends are dead.

I have only one thing I can use to escape—my mind. They have no idea of my psychic ability. If I can think of a way to get us out of here, my piloting skills are strong enough that if I steal a ship I can get us off this planet. The odds are not in our favor, but I can't give up.

I slacken my jaw, loosen my muscles, and give every impression I've surrendered. The less the guards pay attention to me the better. I don't need to read the Emperor's mind to know where he's taking Grace—either his bedroom or the dungeon. I shiver, then strengthen my resolve to figure this out. My sweet Grace couldn't tolerate either of those.

Grace, I thrust my thoughts at her. Amara, *I'm trying to think of a way out of this, but things don't look good.*

Oh my God, Tyree. I'm afraid. Did you see the expression on his face? He's going to kill you!

Don't worry about me. Grace, I've looked inside his mind. He's a monster. Grab the paring knife near your plate. No one's paying attention to you. Do it now! Good. You don't want to hear this, but if I can't get us out of here you may want to use it on yourself.

What are you saying?

They're talking, Amara, I need to pay attention to what they're saying.

That had to have scared the *drack* out of her, but death by her own hand would be a far better fate than what awaits her as part of his slave harem like that poor girl in her cell.

"Take him to the killing room in the dungeon. Secure him to the wall. I think the lady and I will watch. It will get us in the mood before I take her to my bedroom." He turns to Grace and asks, "Would that please you, my lady? Seeing your lover die by my own hand?"

"He's not my lover," she protests. Good, the more she distances herself from me the better. It might save her life.

"I've watched you together. I have my doubts about that. Guards, let's move."

In all the confusion transporting us out of his suite, no one notices my wrist comm light up. The ship! I press the face of the comm against my thigh so the light attracts no attention. I hope it's Shadow. And I hope to every God in the heavens that my psychic powers have increased enough for me to accomplish everything I need to do.

I push my thoughts up through the ceiling, through the roof, and up into the atmosphere to Shadow's signature. I had to establish a mental link with him two *lunars* ago when we took over our vessel and killed our captors. I was little Tyree then, and he was an asshole whom I hated. I have more powers now, and we have an almost-brotherly bond. My mind strains to reach him.

Shadow. Shadow. Shadow. Please. My life depends on this. Grace's life depends on this. *Shadow!*

What, brother? How are you in my mind?

It doesn't matter. Listen closely! The Emperor is a madman, a sadist, and he's dragging us to his dungeon to kill me, then...harm Grace. He said you all were dead. I guess he exaggerated?

We outran MarZan and doubled back here. Glad we had time to repair our hyperdrive. We've got to get you two off the planet before they find us here.

Shadow, can you touch down and come to the concert hall? We're going to be underneath the very rooms we've been sleeping in. I'm hoping my telepathic powers can disable the eight guards who are pointing their weapons at us. We can make a run for it, return to the ship, then leave atmo.

All that and avoid capture by the three MarZan ships that are on our tail? Sounds easy, Tyree.

I realize I'm asking you and the others to risk your lives on a fool's errand. If it weren't for Grace, I'd tell you to leave me behind.

I call you brother now, Tyree. And I still owe Grace more than I can calculate. I'll be there. I'll get two volunteers. Give me the coordinates.

I'll keep our mind link open, Shadow. I'll need to know when you're close by so I can try to disable them at the perfect time.

They're dragging us down several flights of steps to the dungeon. This place was built eons ago with stone and mortar. It's dank, filthy, and poorly lit. I'm surrounded by the Emperor's cadre of guards. He and Grace are behind me. I psychically reach out to her, but I'm hit by a wall of terror so impenetrable I can't get through.

My pulse is pounding in fear. This plan, flimsy as it is, has a thousand moving parts and little to no chance of working. It hinges on psychic powers I'm not sure I possess. I would need to overpower the minds of every male in this room—all at once. The timing with Shadow would have to be flawless.

I feel like an idiot when I realize I don't have to disable nine people. All I have to do is crawl into the Emperor's mind and have him order his men to stand down and release us. I try to slip into his mind like I did yesterday, but I can't get in.

Instead of sliding in like smoke, I push harder, attempting to force my way inside his thoughts. I have no luck. Perhaps it's his high state of emotion—the bloodlust, the arousal—but nothing I try gains me access. Now I worry if I can overpower even one of the guards, much less eight of them. I hate to admit I'm losing hope, but I am.

I hear soft crying from down the hall. I assume it's Tawny, the human female I saw in my mind's eye, probably locked in her cell. The sadistic *Suratan* is probably down here, too. The evil bastard. If I do get off this planet, I vow to kill the Emperor and that demonic *Suratan*, Devolose.

"Chain him facing the wall," the Emperor orders. I can sense the giddy excitement in his voice. I was inside his mind long enough yesterday to know with certainty that he isn't going to kill me quickly. It's going to be a long, painful affair.

I put up no fight, what would be the point? They chain my wrists so high above my head my shoulders strain in their sockets. My ankles are cuffed tightly with my feet spread wide.

"Cut off his clothes," the Emperor commands. "Having fun, Grace? We're only getting started."

"Get your hands off me." I hear what sounds like Grace slapping idly at the Emperor. Then I hear a much harder slap, and Grace grunting in pain.

I can't do anything for her right now. He's not going to kill her. The next few hours are going to provide far too much enjoyment for that. I need to put my attention on the task at hand, which is to keep my wits about me and endure whatever his minions do to me until Shadow tells me he's nearby. Then will I be able to disable all these men? Have I brought three comrades here only to be slaughtered by the Emperor's guards?

Even though I've been expecting it, I'm still startled by the sound of Mauritious' whip singing through the air, and then the pain of many strips of leather landing on my back. Agony sears through every nerve ending. The pain is hot and ex-cruciating.

The level of difficulty of this mission just increased by ten-fold. How do I use these brand new psychic powers when all of my conscious effort needs to be directed at tolerating this torture?

I'll concentrate on what I'm grateful for. I'm thankful I'm not facing Grace. That would be too much to bear. If I was looking at her and had to see that asshole's handprint reddening her cheek, I would be far too focused on revenge, and I'd never get us out of here.

I hear the sound of the whip whistling toward me again. I draw my thoughts out of my head and into Mauritious'. Getting into his mind seems like child's play. I have a glimmer of hope. My plan has a slim chance of working, although I don't know what will happen if all eight guards are disabled but the Emperor is not. I don't know if he's armed. Perhaps since he's always surrounded by his personal protection squad, he doesn't carry a weapon of his own.

I'm in Mauritious' body, looking out through his eyes. It is my hand on the lash. I see Tyree's back, covered in thin ribbons of red. A few stripes of blood have trickled all the way down his ass to his thighs.

I vow not to look in Grace's direction. I would come undone if I did. I look elsewhere and count eight guards, including the one in which I'm currently residing. I wield the whip toward the naked back of the fellow shackled to the wall. I slow my hand, administering less pain than the previous two strikes. Tyree makes no sound, nor does he flinch.

"Halt!" commands the Emperor. "The bastard has passed out already. After only two blows with the whip of ten tails. Weak little piece of shit. Throw a bucket of water on him."

I slip back into my own form so my body will react to the water. I stay there for the next strike of the lash. I've never experienced this level of pain. Grace's cries and pleas for leniency don't make this any easier; my fear for her is overwhelming.

I can do this. I can withstand the pain. I'm certain every male on the ship has been through worse. The female down the hallway has suffered worse. I can and will do anything necessary to free my female.

I dart back into the torturer's body and manipulate him into administering lighter blows. I pop back into my body after the stroke has landed, then groan and writhe in agony. I *am* in agony, still wearing the flesh of my body, but at least I avoid the blows themselves.

"That's ten, your Highness. Certainly, you've punished him enough?"

I hadn't realized I'd already endured ten lashings, but it pains me more to hear Grace's sweet lips pleading with that monster.

Tyree, I'm down the street from the concert hall. I'm here with Steele and Dax. Tell me how to get to you.

I give the directions. *Shadow, I'm going to try to disable all nine of them—eight guards and the Emperor. I've never attempted anything nearly this ambitious. If I do get control of all of them, I'm certain I can only do so for a few modicums, perhaps a* minima *at most. Give the signal "now" through our mindlink when you're at the top of the steps. I'll try to immobilize them. I'll say "abort" if I can't accomplish it. If you hear that word, promise me you'll get back to the ship and leave us behind. Grace has a tiny knife. I've told her to take her own life. She won't have to suffer. Save yourselves. I don't want to lure you three to your deaths on a fool's errand.*

Drack you, brother. I'm not leaving you or Grace to die in a dungeon. The next word you hear from me will be "now."

I feel the full force of the lash, twice in excruciatingly quick succession. I shouldn't have wasted my effort trying to convince Shadow to leave us here. He's a good male; he'd never do that. He, Steele, and Dax will die trying to help us. I hope they don't have to.

I hear Grace slap away the Emperor's hand, then his maniacal laugh. I hope he's the first one Shadow kills.

Grace! Shadow and the males are here. If you have the chance, run to a corner, or down the hall. Flee to safety. Get ready. Any moment now.

Now! I hear Shadow's voice and pull all of my attention to this moment. My mind reaches out to nine minds at once. The guards are easy. I don't feel any resistance from them. The whip has stopped moving. Their raucous enjoyment of the 'entertainment' has ceased. I'm certain they're all paralyzed.

I hear three sets of boots pounding down uneven steps, even as I search for the Emperor's mind signature. The sound of laserfire greets me, then I hear heavy bodies hitting the ground. I'm too focused on my task to count, I just know that several of their minds flickered out of existence, like a flame sputtering when doused with water.

I cast my mind to where the Emperor had been sitting. I try to find his depraved thoughts, but he's not there.

"Guards are all dead, Tyree." It's Shadow. "Dax, shoot them all again, I don't want to take any chances. Where's Grace? And the Emperor?"

"Unlock these shackles. I can't find the Emperor's individual signal." I'm frantic, trying to find Grace or the Emperor's minds. I locate Grace but my connection's weak.

"Dax, use the laser to cut those chains," Shadow orders, his tone sharp, serious.

The tension loosens on my wrists and ankles and I step away from the wall. Grabbing a gun from a dead guard's hand, I move to the left down the hall, toward Grace's faint thoughts. She's easy to find in the middle of the hallway that runs along the cells. She's in her white dress, one sleeve ripped almost completely off. Hunched over a still form, her arm arcs up over her head then slashes down into the body—again and again.

Quirinus is beneath her, clearly dead. As I approach, I observe his glassy, unseeing eyes and realize why I couldn't find his thoughts—he has none.

Grace is still stabbing his lifeless form, repeating "Fuck you," over and over. With each thrust, she calls him another odious Earth epithet. The spray of his red blood has marked her white gown from hem to breast. Her face is almost bathed in it, and yet her arm will not stop piercing that little paring knife into his chest, his arms, and his throat.

"Grace?" I lean into her line of sight to grab her attention. "Grace? He's dead, sweet."

Her arm doesn't slow, nor do the curse words.

"Bastard." Stab. "Asshole." Stab. "Motherfucker." Stab. Then back to "Fuck you," again and again.

"Grace. It's me, Tyree. I'm safe. You're safe. We need to leave and get back to the *Warrior*."

This seems to bring her out of her trance. She looks down at her hands, literally bathed in blood. She glances at the body on the floor in front of her and shudders. "He's dead?" Her hand still clutches the knife, at the ready in case he comes back to life.

"Dead, *Amara*. Dead. Can you run? We'll need to hurry back to the ship."

"Not far," Shadow informs us. "Savannah's piloting a hovercraft around the corner. Said it was child's play to fly. Not fifty steps from the door."

"I can walk. We're safe?" Her eyes seem huge in her blood-spattered face.

"We will be as soon as we're back on board our vessel, Grace." I stroke her back and help her to her feet. She's completely dazed.

"Dax, Steele, can you get her to the craft? Shadow and I have one more thing we need to do."

Shadow lifts his eyebrow in silent question. I watch as the two gladiators escort Grace up the first two steps, then see Dax scoop her into his arms and carry her the rest of the way. I feel no jealousy. She needs the help.

"There's an Earth female down this hall. She's in bad shape. We're rescuing her." I'll brook no argument. We're taking her with us even if Shadow objects.

He doesn't say a word in protest, just follows me. The female's nearby, squatting in the corner of her cell, nude. The evil *Suratan* is in the cell with her.

"Shadow, keep your gun trained on the male. Shoot him if he moves one muscle."

I turn to the female, my voice calm and steady. "We're here to take you away. You'll be safe. We won't harm you." She looks at us, her eyes wide in fear, yet no questions pass her lips. "You'll be safe," I repeat. "Come with us."

She doesn't rise from her crouch. Her face barely registers that we're speaking to her—offering her freedom. I stay where I am and reach out a hand. I thought this would reassure her, but she flinches backward, crossing her arms at the wrists in front of her face.

Shadow tries, his tone soft. "You're from Earth. There are Earth women on the ship. They'll help you. You'll have your own room, your own door. With a lock."

She blinks rapidly, still fearful, but she lowers her arms to her sides.

"The Emperor's dead. He won't be able to come after you. But we have to hurry. Please," my tone is urgent.

She stands but is still huddled in the corner. I think it was the word 'please' that penetrated her paralysis.

"Okay." She takes a step toward us, but I motion her back.

"We need to use the laser to break you out."

The laser easily cuts through the rusted metal and I reach my hand out again. "Quickly. Please. We'll all be killed if we don't hurry."

"Yes, I'll come with you. Only if Devi comes, too."

She quit moving; she's waiting for our agreement.

"Devi? Another female?"

Every *modicum* that passes increases our chances of getting caught. Grace isn't safe out there. We have to leave in a *dracking* hurry. If there's another female we can grab her and run.

She shakes her head. "Devi." She points with her chin at the demonic male who shares her cell.

There he is. The *Suratan* from my childhood. Standing still as a statue, an unreadable expression on his face.

"Devolose has to come with us." This frail, battered female's voice is firm.

There's no time. Absolutely no time to argue. Many people's lives are at stake. I don't have one more *modicum* to argue with her. I either take them both, or rescue neither. I can't leave her in this cell.

"I know what you did," I threaten, my voice low and serious, directed at the demon. "My gun will be pointed at you every step you take. If you so much as go one *ince* out of line I will kill you without a moment's hesitation." I have no idea why she wants him with us. Maybe so she can choke the life from his useless body with her own hands.

"Not an *ince* out of line, do you understand?"

He nods once, his face still completely without expression.

We head back down the hall, the demon in front of me, my laser on full power. The girl is in Shadow's arms, one hand under her knees, one around her torso, and her head on his chest.

The hovercraft is waiting for us at the corner. We quickly squeeze in, the demon across from me, my weapon openly aimed at his chest. I take one moment to glance at Grace, her face is covered in blood, but she's still in one piece. Then I put my full attention on the devil I was warned about in my childhood.

Chapter Fourteen

Tyree

We made it to the ship and left atmo so fast it was almost like a dream. I could feel the vessel lurch into hyperdrive almost immediately. At least Grace's concerts paid for that. Axxios is an excellent pilot, the Emirusian navy won't be able to find us, nor will the cartel. We're safe when we're flying; it's just when we land for supplies that we have to worry.

The rescued female and the devil were taken to medbay by a contingent of five gladiators. I'm with Grace in her room. She's still in a daze as I peel her filthy blood-soaked dress off her and help her into the shower. I look down and realize I'm nude—it doesn't matter. I stash the huge red gemstone necklace in a drawer, I'm not sure why, then run the dress to the garbage jettison bay. I know she'll never want to see that bloody reminder again.

She's finishing her shower when I return to her room. I help her into a t-shirt and panties, then jump into the shower. She didn't want to leave my side, so she's sitting on the toilet with her head in her hands.

"That was so terrible," she tells me when I'm toweling dry. "I couldn't bear to see Mauritious hit you with that whip. I felt every sting of the lash myself."

I startle. Those sound like the words of a truemate. I'm certain it's just an Earth expression; I caution myself not to get my hopes up.

When I was under the spray of the water, my pain was deadened. Now that I'm dry, my back is on fire. I glance over my shoulder at the mirror and can't believe what I see. My skin is shredded. It doesn't even look humanoid. I do the math; Grace mentioned ten lashes well before the torture was complete. Ten strikes with a whip of ten tails—there are over one hundred slashes on my back, buttocks, and thighs.

"Tyree, you need to go to medbay. Let's have Dr. Drayke treat your wounds and give you something for the pain."

"Yes, *Amara*. I'll go—after you're asleep."

"I'll be fine. You need to go to medbay now."

"Let's watch that vid of the snow bear of planet Zath you found so boring. As soon as you're asleep I'll go. I promise."

"No. I'll go with you so you don't have to worry about me."

I don't want her anywhere near that devil, so I compromise and tuck her into bed. "I'll go straight to the doc, Grace. I'll come back as soon as I'm patched up."

I put on a loincloth—even that small scrap of fabric pressed against my flesh feels like needles of fire—then wend my way to medbay.

Doc's in a private exam room with the female. Five armed gladiators are squeezed into another room with the devil. I guess I'll have to wait my turn for the doc to treat my back. I won't feel comfortable until that animal is locked in the cellblock deep in the belly of the ship.

Dr. Drayke leaves Tawny's exam room and steps into the hall with Shadow and me. He is the calmest, most logical male on the ship. I've never heard a sharp or unkind word from him. I've also never seen this particular expression on his blue face. His lips are pressed together so tightly they're quivering.

"I'm just about done here. I just…I just needed…" His words sputter to a stop. He glances at the floor, then whispers, "I may need you to physically restrain me. I'm having very vivid fantasies of killing the male in the next room with my scalpel. That is strictly forbidden by my Lord God Anteros. Why is that devil on board this vessel?"

"She wouldn't leave the dungeon without him. We didn't have time to inquire about her reasons."

"I've never seen anything this disturbing in my career," he whispers to us. "Bruises in every stage of healing, from fresh to weeks old, indicating severe and chronic abuse. Particular attention was paid to her…sexual parts."

He looks at the door to the devil's room as if he could stare through it. "She tells me that animal did most of it. And she wouldn't come here without him?"

"If you can get her patched up, let's do it, doc. We'll get him in a cell and escort her to a cabin near the females where she can heal and feel safe. I plan on speaking with Zar. I think we'll need to conduct a tribunal. Death doesn't seem too small a punishment."

"Indeed," the doctor says, lips compressed in a thin line. We accompany him into the room where he finishes applying salve and plas-film to fresh wounds on her back. She's huddled under a thin blanket covering her chest and legs.

"We'll call Anya and Zoey to medbay and have them bring clothes and show you to your new cabin. It's bright and clean and comfortable. You'll be safe there," the doc says in an attempt to sound upbeat and cheery.

"I won't go without Devi." Her jaw is stiff. She looks adamant.

The doc's eyes widen in shock. Evidently, he didn't understand the part about "she wouldn't leave without him" when we told him the story.

"Surely you know he needs to be locked up," the doc explains rationally.

"Okay. I'm used to that. Can you put us in the same cell, though?" Her voice is resigned, almost without hope.

"Perhaps you don't understand. *You* don't need to be in a cell. Just him. You said he did this to you, correct?"

"Yes, much of it."

"This is illegal and immoral and will require punishment, Tawny. *He* needs to be locked in a cell. *You* do not."

She shakes her head and lies on her side on the table. "Please don't separate us," is all she says, before pulling the covers over her head.

The doc finishes with her and leaves the room, advising her to get some sleep. "I know your back needs attention, Tyree, and according to the rules of triage, you should be attended to next. But I'd like to give that male a quick exam and get him in a cell, then take care of you. Any objections?"

"I agree. Get him the *drack* out of here."

Shadow and I squeeze into the small exam room crammed with Devolose and five other gladiators. The doc gives him a perfunctory once-over. Even though I have to peek between two comrades, I can see welts and scars all over the male's red-and-black flesh. All I can think is, "good, he deserves it. That and more."

"Take off your loincloth," the doctor directs, unable to keep his loathing out of his tone.

For the first time since I've seen this male, I observe something that passes for emotion flit across his impassive face. His hands are slow as he unties the cloth, then pulls it away from his body. Every male in the room flinches.

"Gods!" Steele hisses as his head jerks back involuntarily.

There is an ugly, badly-healed wound where his penis has been severed from his body. There is a small hole I assume he pisses out of. To say the appearance is shocking is an understatement. I feel the slightest moment of compassion for the poor bastard, then conjure up images of the things he did to the girl in the next room. He deserved it.

Dr. Drayke gives the area a cursory examination with his gloved hands. "Having trouble urinating?" he inquires dispassionately.

The devil shakes his head no.

"You may put your clothing back on."

Shadow and I leave the room and make another attempt to convince Tawny to go to the cabin already prepared for her. She got so upset arguing with us, we finally acquiesced, and the gladiators escorted them both to a cell.

I'm in an exam room with the doc. "Most of these cuts will heal well, Tyree, but there were a few places where the flesh was shredded so badly I needed to apply medskin. It will adhere to your existing flesh and eventually mesh with it."

He applies an analgesic salve, which puts an immediate end to the fiery pain, then places a layer of plas-film over the top.

"You'll mend fine, Tyree. You're a good male. You saved Miss Grace. I know it's none of my business, but...you care for her a great deal, don't you?"

"I want her to be my mate," I tell him seriously, looking him in the eye.

He smiles for the first time today. "You two are good together. I'm so glad for you both."

"Don't get too excited, doc. She's not on board with the plan."

Grace

I was in a sleep filled with dreams of dark dungeons, pain, and claustrophobia. And blood, rivers of blood. Tyree enters my cabin quietly, but I startle awake, glad to be out of that dreamworld.

"Tyree, how's your back?"

"It will heal. More important, how are you, Grace? You've been through so much."

I don't know what to say. I think I'm in shock, and God knows <u>he</u> should be, just look at his back, it's cut to ribbons.

"Get some sleep, Tyree. Lie with me."

"I'm surprised you'd want a male anywhere near you after..."

"You used the right word before when you called him a monster. Not all males are like that. You're not. You saved my life. I don't know how you did it."

"I've got more psychic power than I thought. I paralyzed all the guards. Evidently, it didn't work against the Emperor. For him, I used a different magical ability—you, Grace."

I'm quiet for a moment. What happened in that hallway is kind of a blur. I don't even want to recall everything, but I remember enough. I understand the word 'bloodlust' now.

"Yeah, I don't know how I feel about that. I killed a person, Tyree. If you'd asked me a few months ago the likelihood of me killing another human being, the answer would have been zero."

"He wasn't a human being, *Amara*. He was an animal. A feral one. It was kill or be killed. You did what had to be done. Without your quick response, we might all be dead."

"Thankfully, I don't remember exactly what happened after he pulled me out of my seat and dragged me down the hallway. I do remember I couldn't stop stabbing him."

He slides in next to me, smoothes my hair away from my face, then kisses my cheek. "He would have killed you,

Grace. You had to kill him first. You did what had to be done. I'm so proud of your strength. To think that a few days ago you were afraid of performing. Now you're a female to be reckoned with."

I feel a chuckle rumble deep in his chest. "The males will be afraid of pissing you off; they'll avoid you in the hallways. After cursing out the Captain of the MarZan ship, and what you did to the Emperor, your name will be spoken in hushed tones with both fear and admiration." He tousles my hair. "My *Amara*. Get some sleep. I'm right here."

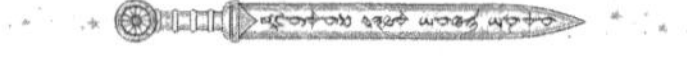

I AWAKEN WITH A start the next morning. I was having nightmarish memories of what happened yesterday. I open my eyes to Tyree's poor, lacerated back. Dear Lord, he went through so much.

I replay those awful moments yesterday when the captain of the guard was flaying Tyree's back with that hideous whip. There was so much going on: fear for Tyree, terror for my own life, as well as the Emperor pawing my breasts with that evil look in his eye. But the thought that was uppermost in my mind much of the time?

My concern for Tyree, more even than for myself.

I care deeply for Tyree. Why I came to this epiphany a moment away from death in a dungeon, I don't know. I must be the densest female in the galaxy.

My stomach feels like it's eating itself in anxiety as I admit to myself just how deeply I'm connected to him.

Tyree's shaggy golden mane calls to me, but I restrain my fingers from combing through his hair. All these tender feelings, all the caring and concern I have for him, and the fact that part of me wants to wake him with kisses—they mean nothing.

Because the other half of me still pictures my mom watching her boyfriends hurt me, then turning a blind eye in order to keep them in her life. I never want to be that weak. I never want to give that much of myself away, and if I tell Tyree how much I like him it will give him power over me. I'll never let that happen.

So I keep my hand at my side. I don't wake this beautiful man with my kisses. I don't offer to go get him breakfast because he's got to be in pain and he just saved my fucking life. I'm having an intense internal argument with myself, taking both sides in a debate about going with my heart or following my better judgment.

The last time he and I talked, Tyree said he'd never bring up the truemate thing again. Even though we slept in the same bed last night, he'd never presume I've changed my mind, he knows me well enough for that. I feel terrible for this, but I'm certain we just need a clean break.

I've never been so happy to hear a knock at the door in my life.

Thank goodness Callista has perfect timing. I pull the sheet up to Tyree's waist, tug my t-shirt down, and rush to answer the door.

"Sorry to bother you, but it's after lunch..." She's standing just inside the threshold, and by the look on her face, she didn't expect to see my bed occupied by the hunkiest male on the ship. "I can see you're busy, I'll come back later."

"No, that's okay," listen to how casual I sound. You'd think I'd been a consummate liar my entire life. "What's up?"

"I've never been a busybody before, but I just can't sit by and watch this happen."

"What are you talking about?"

"The girl you two liberated, Tawny. Dr. Drayke says she was badly beaten and abused by that asshole you brought on board. Thank goodness he's locked up tight in the cell block where we were imprisoned before the rebellion. But are you aware she won't leave him? She refused to even look at the cabin we prepared for her. Right now she's sleeping in one of those horrible cells. With him!" She steps farther into the room and paces in tight little circles near the door.

"It's clearly Stockholm Syndrome, Grace. I've got to help her understand she isn't bound to that devil! I want to get her out of the cellblock and away from him and his influence. She doesn't know me from Adam. You rescued her. Perhaps she trusts you. Come with me. Help me talk some sense into her."

I'm a quiet person. I've never tried to persuade anyone to do anything. I'm a horrible choice for this job. However, I'd give anything to leave my room right now, to avoid any difficult discussions with Tyree. He's still lying in bed, his back toward the door, although he has to be awake by now.

"Well, if you really think I could be of service...I'd be happy to help. Have a seat. I'll be out of the shower and completely dressed in five minutes."

I know she didn't believe my time frame, but I'm dressed, my wet hair pulled into a ponytail in less than seven minutes. Before I leave, I set Tyree's clothes in a neat pile on the bed. I hope it's a clear message for him to vacate before I return.

A few minutes later, my jaw tenses as we enter the hallway connected to the cell block. My God, this brings back horrifying memories. I'd contemplated suicide every waking hour for days on end when I was here two months ago. I felt so alone, so isolated, so hopeless. My life is immeasurably better now—partially due to Tyree. He's a terrific male. I enjoy him so much.

I think of our silly food fight the other day. He even makes watching boring vids fun. And he's so solicitous about my needs and wants...and desires. Too bad he's stuck on this truemate thing. I simply can't give away my self, my autonomy.

My fear ratchets up ten notches after we cross the threshold of the cellblock, and it goes through the roof when the door closes behind me. The hair on the back of my neck stands on end. Callista looks at me, white showing all the way around her eyes—she feels it, too.

"You sure we want to do this?" I ask. "I hope it goes fast, I can't wait to get out of here."

"Me, too. But let's give it our best shot, Grace. The girl is young and scared and obviously confused. We have to try to get her out of his clutches."

They're both in the third cell; the one Anya and Zar occupied. This is where their love bloomed. It strikes me that Tawny and the red-and-black devil should be in any cell but this.

It looks like someone allowed them to drag a second mattress in there. Both beds are pulled together on the floor. Tawny and the devil look like they're spooning under the covers. Bile rises in my throat as I picture being in that position with one of the Urluts, the boar-like aliens who kidnapped me from Earth. I can't imagine wanting one of them near me, much less touching me. Unlike this bastard, they never laid a hand on me and certainly never tortured me.

"Tawny? Remember me? We didn't get introduced, but I'm Grace. I helped you escape."

She rises from the bed, steps over the devil lying next to her and stands a foot inside the bars across from us. "You killed the Emperor. I watched you stab him until your arm was too tired to move."

I feel Callista's eyes bore into me. I suppose it *is* kind of shocking for her to know that quiet, unassuming Grace stabbed that motherfucker so many times she was drenched in his blood.

"Yes. No one should allow themselves to be treated badly. If someone hurts us, we should rise up if we have the means to do so." I wait, hoping to see awareness and agreement dawn on her beautiful, bruised face—nothing.

"I'm Cally. I was a prisoner in one of these cells a few months ago, Tawny. We rebelled. We defeated our captors. None of them will torment us anymore."

She looks at us, eyes empty, with zero comprehension.

Cally goes on, pointedly glancing at the male on the floor, then back at Tawny. "I'm not a psychiatrist or anything, but I think you're suffering from Stockholm Syndrome."

Tawny shakes her head, her features tight, "I don't know what you're talking about."

"I don't remember all the specifics, but I think patrons at a bank were held hostage by some bad guys and at the end of the ordeal they wanted to protect their captors. They named a syndrome after it to show that sometimes people get their thoughts turned around when they've been in grave danger. They think the aggressor is their friend."

Tawny shrugs, looking clueless.

"You admitted to Dr. Drayke that he," Cally points at him, almost as if she's a witness in a courtroom drama, "tortured and abused you, yet you want to stay in this horrid cell with him. We have a lovely cabin in a wing of this ship where all of us women live. We'd love to be friends. We want to help you. We don't understand why you're sleeping on the floor with a male who hurt you."

"I don't know you. I don't know either of you. I know Devi. I want to stay with him." Her shoulders pull back, her chest thrusts out, her jaw is rigid. "I'm *not* confused. I don't *have* Stockholm Syndrome. I'm staying right here." She points at the floor. "With Devi."

Cally's mouth works although no words come out. Her eyes shine brightly with unshed tears. "Tawny. Think about what you're doing. He's not safe."

"I don't have to explain things to you. I don't owe you anything." She takes a deep breath, glancing back at the male who's under the covers behind her. "I have no idea how long I was in captivity. What year is it?"

Her eyes widen in shock when we tell her. "I was in his clutches for three years." She shivers in repulsion for a moment, absorbing the enormity of that fact. "There are only two living people who know what happened during those...what, thousand days? Only the two people on this side of these bars know the truth. I'm staying here." With that, she turns on her heel and steps over the prone figure on the floor. She climbs under the blanket she shares with her abuser and turns her back to us.

"I'll be back, Tawny," Cally says, her voice strong and firm. "You'll see the truth when you give it some thought. You're just all turned around inside."

Silence.

We exit the cell block.

"Not exactly the outcome we'd hoped for," I tell Cally.

"My heart hurts for her. She's totally brainwashed." Cally shakes her head sadly.

"It will just take time. We'll help her see the truth, and when she does, we'll bring that bastard to justice."

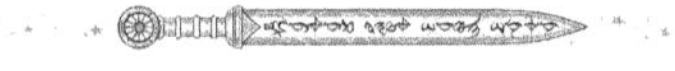

I GRAB SOME LUNCH from the dining area and bring it back to my cabin. I hope Tyree got my hint and cleared out.

He made the bed and left absolutely no trace of himself in my room. Maybe it's better that way.

I sit on the little chair in the corner, eating a mystery meat sandwich. Maddie called it *Crayton Dergar*, but it was barely edible and the fancy name was like putting lipstick on a pig—it didn't dress up the taste.

It's quiet in here. Too quiet. I don't like the silence. I miss Tyree's jokes and, frankly, I miss his presence.

I can't help but think about Tawny. How pathetic. Her resemblance to my mom irritates me. I don't like weak women. She's giving up her happiness, her comfort, her safety, for what? To please a man Tyree described as an abusive monster?

That's spineless and pitiful, and I try not to have sympathy for her—but I do. I feel sorry for her neediness, her willingness to sell her soul for approval from that despicable male. I never want to do that.

My thoughts stop. They grind to a halt like when a stick is thrown into the gears of a machine. Although I have crystal clarity about why I don't want to be Tyree's truemate, that whole line of thinking doesn't make sense anymore.

I review my concerns: I don't want to give up pieces of myself to please anyone. Riiight.

Then I page through the book labeled <u>Tyree</u> in my mind. I look at every chapter, every scene of every minute we've spent together, from when he was three-foot-tall little female elf Tyree, to big, strapping gorgeous muscular Tyree. From watching vids during a sleepover, to throwing food in the kitchen, to fighting for our lives on Emirus, to making love on that bed.

The bed stares at me accusingly. I stare back. Then I return to paging through my <u>Tyree</u> book. I'm looking closely, but I can't find one chapter or page or paragraph where he tried to take *me* away from *me*. I can't find one sentence where he told me what to do or asked something of me that wasn't in my best interests. Not. One.

The only tense moment between the two of us was about my inability to say I didn't want to eat the sack of shit. And the tension was because he was encouraging me to speak up for myself—the opposite of telling me what to do.

He risked his life to stay behind and save Tawny. He was more worried about my safety than his own in that dungeon when he was practically being flayed alive. This man would never, ever want me to do anything that wasn't good for me. How did he describe a truemate? Linked, connected, eternally joined. Would that be so terrible? Really?

My breath huffs out as it dawns on me, not in tiny increments, but in one big avalanche—I love him. I love him and he loves me. He said it. He's shown it—over and over in fact—repeatedly, and in many ways.

How long would it have taken me if I had dated Barbarian, or Rocky, or Butch or any of the guys my mother went out with to figure out they were assholes? Less than an hour.

How long would it take to figure out the male in the cell with Tawny is a devil? A minute—just look at him.

I'm not stupid, or gullible. I'm smart. I'm smart enough to discern a good male from a bad one. And I'm smart enough to know I'm in love with Tyree—and he would never hurt me.

If there's anything I learned in that fucking dungeon, it's that life is short. I could spend the next week or month or year debating and wondering about this decision—I would have done that in my old life. But the new Grace is resolute and strong. I have all the information I need to make a decision—in fact, the decision's already been made!

Chapter Fifteen

I tolerated about half an *houra* alone in my room after I left Grace's. I'm just learning who I am, and I'm still not sure of a lot about myself now that I'm male. But I do know I'm not the type to sit around and stay idle or feel self-pity.

I'm in the *ludus*, practicing with the chainsticks. I know I'll get better at fighting and sparring, although how could I compete with anyone in this vessel full of gladiators? However, I'll never be good at these *dracking* sticks. Shadow chided me for not paying attention, but I was paying complete attention, and all I have to show for it is a lump on my jaw the size of an *oreg* egg.

"Are you sure you don't want to go eat or watch a vid, Tyree? You're useless here. If you don't pay better attention, you're going to kill yourself...or an innocent bystander," Shadow scolds.

"I *am* paying attention."

"You told me what happened with you and Grace on Emirus. She rejected you and you're mooning over her. If you were paying full attention to your martial arts, why are you sprouting an erection?"

I look down and sheepishly see the evidence for all to see. Okay, maybe I wasn't paying complete attention to those *dracking*, deadly chainsticks. What purpose are they supposed to serve anyway?

My thoughts drift to Grace. I'm not wallowing in self-pity in my room for a reason. I'm a male of action. I'm not going to sit back and wait for fate to fix things for me. I'm struck by an image of the mating behavior of the *nygrin* birds on Larian. I used to watch them as a child.

The males would bring the females the choicest bits of food, and the females would fly away, not even tasting the morsels. The males would just repeat this behavior for days, trying with every instinct they had to please the female. They wouldn't give up even though as a child I couldn't understand why they kept trying. After a while, I realized that eventually they always got rewarded.

I'm not giving up. I know what pleases Grace. I will keep approaching her with things I know she likes. I'll persist in letting her see my love for her shining through. I have all the time in the galaxy. We're stuck on this ship together. I'll keep being my best self for her. She'll have to eventually realize we'll be amazing together.

The *ludus* suddenly goes silent. No sound of grunting or sparring, no loud clang of metal weights hitting the floor. Every eye in the room focuses on the door, then slides to me, and then back to the door.

I slowly swivel to see Grace in that gorgeous green dress. The eye-popping dress she said matches my eyes. The sexy dress that's been deprived of the modest covering of black lace at her bust and shows far too much of her heaving bosom. She was correct when she complained that the dress was cut so low her breasts would spill out the top.

I want to threaten the males with death if they spend one more *modicum* drinking in the sight of her. But I don't want to turn my back on her to accomplish that.

She seems unaware of my protective anger as she hurries toward me, then stands far too close for comfort. At my vantage point, I can't help looking down into the vee of her dress. She was right, you can see a hint of the pink of her nipples peeking from beneath the threshold of the top.

"Tyree, can we talk?"

I'm a complete *drack*. Any male worth the air he breathes wouldn't be stealing peeks at her breasts. I force my eyes to her face. She looks serious and...so many emotions swirling there I have no way of discerning what's going on behind her large blue eyes.

"Certainly." I'm still standing, paralyzed. I think my heart stopped beating in my chest. I can't read her—don't know what she wants.

"Tyree!" Shadow yells from the other side of the weights. "Get the *drack* out of here. Go with that female unless you want to mount her right here in front of every male on the ship."

His words propel me forward; I take Grace's elbow and escort her out the double doors into the hallway. Then I stop. Like when a machine runs out of fuel. I just stand there, as if waiting for direction.

"Could we...could we go somewhere private to talk?" Grace asks.

I'm still not moving. My brain has shut down.

"Like your room? Or my room? Or the solarium?"

I love the solarium. Even when it's empty, to me it's still filled with Grace's music. I don't release her elbow—I practically drag her there.

We're here, surrounded on three sides and the ceiling by darkness and stars: there's a purple-tinged nebula off to the right. Grace looks so beautiful I can't tear my eyes from her.

"I'm an idiot—"

"Don't talk like that about the woman I love, Grace. I won't allow it."

"I'm...I had a whole speech planned out, Tyree. I was going to explain myself and tell you my feelings, and beg your forgiveness for being an idi...But then you go and ruin it by being awesome and terrific and telling me you love me even though I'm a dolt."

"You're not a dolt, either. But I'd like to hear more." My heart has unclenched for the first time in days. I think I've gotten a reprieve. I want to hear every word. I slip my hands from her elbows to her naked shoulders and pull her a step closer. I truly want to hear every word. I also want to glance down her dress and see those magnificent breasts rise and fall with every breath she takes.

"I realized I'm not going to lose myself. I can still be Grace even though I'm in a relationship with you. As a matter of fact, in some ways I've found myself. I'm strong. I called Gren names and was ready to go to battle with him. I protected myself on Emirus. I wasn't intimidated by the Emperor. Even before he acted crazy I knew that ten of him wasn't worth one of you, Tyree. You're...magnificent."

Her eyes dart to mine for the first time since she collected me in the *ludus*.

"I can love you—which I do by the way—with all my heart, and not lose myself. You've talked about truemates, but I don't know what that is. Can you explain it?"

"You probably have something like it on Earth, *Amara*. On Larian it's a product of biology. Between you and me it will be a commitment of our souls. I love the idea that this hasn't happened by a simple accident of chemistry—with you and me it's happened by choice. It will be so much more profound.

"It means we love each other and will stay together and work in tandem for what we want. We decide what's good for us as a team and we pull together in the same direction to accomplish it. Our decisions are always mutual. We want what's best for each other. When each of us puts the other first, things always work out.

"Truemates. Forever and always. You'll never be alone. I'll always be by your side." I pierce her with a stare that I hope shows her just how serious I am.

"Oh my God. I want that, Tyree. I want to be with you forever. A team. We'll be amazing. I want to keep sharing everything we've already come to share. Except *sacru sheswah*. That will never cross our threshold, promise me that."

"Quite a speech, Miss Grace. But I happen to like *sacru sheswah*. What if that's a deal-breaker?"

"Then fuck you, Tyree. You told me to ask for what I want. No sack of shit will come within fifty paces of me."

"Good girl, Grace. I love it when you tell me no." I step forward and drop my voice so low it rumbles in my chest. "If I told you to come with me to our room right now, would you tell me no?" My hands reach around her shoulders and pull her closer.

She shakes her head and looks me straight in the eyes.

"If I told you my fantasy from our room on Emirus. My fantasy about the green dress you are wearing right this very *minima*, would you tell me no?" My index finger trails maddeningly slowly from her jaw to her neck, then her collar bone, and finally slides along the dangerously low neckline of her dress.

A brilliant, naughty smile brightens her face as she shakes her head and leans up for my fingers to touch her more intimately. I try to ignore *drackhead's* insistent kick.

"If I wanted to touch you in ways you've never been touched, would you tell me no?" My other hand slowly caresses down her back and rests on the swell of her delicious ass. *Drackhead* is pulsing with excitement.

"No." Her voice is strong, certain, while her smile widens.

"If I were to pull your breasts up and rest them on the top of your dress, so they were on display for me, would you say no?"

"No," her voice is a sexual groan.

I lift one breast and then the other so they are lasciviously propped on top of the material. "My Gods, Grace. Your body is so magnificent."

I dip my head and whisper intimately in her ear. "If I were to nip and suck your pink tips would you want to say no?"

She shakes her head as she sucks in a gasp of air.

I nip the cords of her neck, bite her collarbone, then trail achingly slowly down the mound of her breast to her nipple which is standing hard and proud. I lick then graze it while my hand mimics the action on her other side. I feel her knees dip as she places all her attention on my actions, then steadies herself, her hands on my shoulders.

I switch positions, giving equal attention to the other side. My nostrils flare as I smell her arousal.

"If I were to tell you to open your legs so I could smell you better and have access to your most private places, would you deny me, Grace?"

"I never want to deny you, Tyree," her voice is breathy, full of desire—for me.

"If I were to..." I reach under the hem of her dress and glide my thumbs up from inside her ankle to her knee, then farther to rest near the juncture of her thighs. "If I were to touch you here would you tell me no?"

Her mouth is open, her eyes closed, she's panting. She licks her lips, "No."

"And this," I slip my fingers through her folds, drenching them in her cream. "Would you ask me to stop now?"

"No," her voice is so filled with lust; the sound is barely a word.

"And if my thumb wanted to take this liberty," I gently circle her bud, avoiding a direct touch, just surrounding the edge. "Would you tell me I've gone too far?"

"Never." She shakes her head.

"And if I were to claim you, Grace. If I were to plunge my fingers into your secret place..." I dip a finger into her slick channel, pull it out and drive it in again. "If I were to claim this as mine. If I were to demand no other could trespass here, would you agree?"

"Yes."

"Say it out loud, *Amara*. Tell me no one will ever touch you here. Not ever." I kneel between her legs, then look up and spear her with a serious stare. My heart is galloping, *drackhead* is bucking against my loincloth.

"No one but you, Tyree." She's panting with desire, her pink lips open, her eyelids closed.

I smile, "That's good, *Amara*. Just me...or you, if I tell you to." Her eyes startle wide then slam closed. Her breath hitches.

"Yes, if that's what you want." Her cheeks pinken, making her even more beautiful in my eyes.

"And if I wanted to drive my cock into you until you scream in pleasure? If I were to take you fully in this room right now, under the stars in the sky, would you allow it?

"Yes, Tyree. I'd allow you anything." She opens her legs wider, an invitation.

"Say it again."

"Tyree, I'd allow you anything."

Dear Gods, she's so gorgeous. "Thank you, *Amara*, but I want to hear what you told me earlier, not about your body but about your heart." I stand and gaze into her eyes, telling her volumes without words.

"I love you, Tyree. I want to be with you. I want to sleep in the same bed with you and share your cabin and giggle with laughter and scream in passion. I want to be happy—I deserve it. And that means I deserve you. I also want to make you happy. Forever.

"And right now, this minute, what could I do to make you happy?" her voice purrs low and sexy.

I tuck her breasts back into her dress where they belong, lift her into my arms and stalk back to her cabin. On the way, I whisper all the things I'm going to do to her in that bed tonight and tomorrow and forever.

Grace

He sets me down after we cross the threshold and he's kicked the door closed. He looks at me with all the love and longing one person can have for another. His blazing gaze warms my blood hotter than all those sexy words in the solarium.

I reach for the loincloth at his waist but soon realize I have no idea how to untie the intricate series of twists and knots. He grabs my hands and places them on his shoulders.

"I'm in charge, *Amara*. First, I unwrap you."

His lips brush mine, feather-soft, then harder while he unzips my dress. His hands slide the emerald fabric down my body and the beautiful creation whispers to the ground. I step out from the middle of the silken puddle to stand so close to him my nipples graze his chest. I wore no underwear, I'm fully naked for his inspection.

He groans as he untwines the loincloth from his body. He pulls me to him, every inch of his warm skin is pressed against mine, his cock is pulsing against my midriff.

He nips my lips with his, then his tongue slips out and slides against the seam of my mouth. How exactly does it work that touching me here creates a pull in my clit all the way down there?

My hand begins its journey to his back, to pull him closer, but I encounter the slick feel of plas-film.

"Oh, sorry. Did that hurt?"

"No. Where else would you like to touch me?" He smiles lazily and lifts an eyebrow. "I'm all yours."

"I had lots of ideas in our room on Emirus. Many, many creative ideas. Hmmm, where should I begin?" His cock takes that moment to pulse against my belly. "Oh, I know just the right thing."

I slowly slide to my knees, all the while looking into those luminous emerald eyes that are blazing more brightly than I've ever seen them.

I lick my lips, then grab his thick cock, my head now even with the object of my desire.

"I've wanted this in my mouth for days, Tyree. I want to taste you." My tongue reaches out to lick his blunt tip. I can't control the low moan that escapes me as I catch a taste of him. It's warm and spicy and will forever be labeled in my mind as "Tyree."

Pulling my head back, I survey his length. Hard and bronze and straight, it pulses in my hand as if in approval of my touch. I graze down to the base, then up to the tip. Noticing the thick veins running the length of him, I follow one with my index finger, then my tongue.

"Grace." His eyes are closed, his lips slightly turned up at the edges. I can tell he's totally focused on my touch. I slick back down and then up to the tip again. Then I swirl around the head, first one way, then the other. His hips press toward me as if to ask for more.

Sucking the head into my mouth, I taste him, feeling the texture of his skin on my tongue. I glance up his body to look at him. His head is thrown back in ecstasy. Every muscle in his body straining against his flesh.

Exploring further, I accept more of him in my mouth. I'm clamped tightly around him—feeling all of him, fully surrounding him. I suck, bobbing my head up and down his shaft. He breathes out in a gust, moaning so softly I can barely hear it.

"Gods, Grace!" He pulls out of me, his hands roaming my shoulders, my back, then lodging in my hair. Reaching under my arms, he pulls me to standing and stares at me with a potent mixture of yearning and love.

He's breathing like a racehorse, a sheen of sweat covering his chest. His hands prowl lower, clutch my ass, graze up my sides, then grasp my cheeks, bracketing my face.

"It feels good to be alive, *Amara*. Especially good right this minute."

Tyree

I'm amazed, shocked, thrilled. There were moments in the last few days where I thought I'd be dead, moments I thought Grace didn't like me or want me, moments I thought I'd be alone forever. I'm the luckiest, happiest male in the galaxy.

"I want to make you feel good, Grace."

"I want everything you want to give me, Tyree." She smiles in invitation.

I know lots of things I want to give her. *Drackhead* has some ideas of his own, too.

I pick her up and set her in the middle of the bed like the most delicate flower. I straddle her knees, wanting to see all of her, spread out naked for me, like a buffet. Her beautiful face is flushed from exertion. Her lips are a deeper shade of red from the friction of sucking my cock. Her blonde hair is darker near her scalp because it's damp from physical activity. Those pink-tipped breasts are hard and pointing up at me.

I move one knee between her legs. She immediately presses down and sets up a rhythm, rubbing her little bud against me. She's drenched, sucking my cock aroused her, preparing her body for more intimacy. Knowing this turns *Drackhead* to stone and makes my balls tighten against my body.

All the daydreams I've had about Grace and what I would do to her if I ever got her into bed again involved slow ramping up, exploring, and tasting her in every way. Today is not the day for any of that. Her hands are wildly roaming my sides. Her breathing is ragged—she needs no additional foreplay.

I smile at her and try to ignore *Drackhead* who's pulsing with need.

He's rewarded with a firm clamp, her hand around his girth. She's fisting him. Leisurely at first, then more vigorously.

"Make love to me, Tyree."

I kiss her deeply, over and over, before I place my cock against her opening. It's so slippery and wet—so welcoming. She presses against me, then puts her hands on my ass and pulls me toward her.

I thrust forward until I'm fully seated. This is nothing like our quick coupling the night we feared for our lives, about to be boarded by the Federation. This feeling, right now, is everything I dreamed of and more. To be thoroughly sheathed in my truemate, fully joined, truly connected. This is sexual and primal and the pleasure is exquisite—but it is so much more. The ecstasy is more emotional than physical.

I've seen vids of vigorous *dracking*, males balls deep and pistoning hard into their females. Today is not the day for that. My pace is slow, unhurried. I gaze into my *Amara's* eyes, noting every expression on her lovely face. She asked me to make love to her. I am doing that. I am loving her with every fiber of my being.

I can feel her walls clench. I know she's close. I lean my pelvis against her little button; this extra pressure pushes her right over the edge to her own orgasm. Her face squeezes in pure rapture, her walls clench me tightly, urging me to my own release. I jet into her, feeling intense pleasure as well as an intimate communion with my mate.

The feeling is so powerful, so beyond anything my own hand has ever provided me. It isn't the physical sensations—it's the pure intimacy. The connection with my *Amara*, my true-mate. I love this female and she loves me. It's more than the physical release that is fueling my bliss; it is this profound bond.

"No words, Tyree. I have no words." She puts her arms around my neck, pulls me close and nestles her head against my chest. I roll us over so we're on our sides, lying in each other's embrace. The entrancing sound of her heartbeat and the knowledge she loves me are the last things I'm aware of before I fall asleep.

Chapter Sixteen

I wake the next morning feeling like a happy cat lying in its favorite sunbeam—warm and relaxed and carefree. Last night was amazing. It strikes me that if sex is that mind-altering when we're just beginners, in the future it's going to be transcendent.

What a transformation we've both experienced over the last few months. I've gone from timid barista on Earth to battle-scarred warrior in space. I'm so much stronger now. I handled everything that came my way on Emirus, and I did it like a boss. I can still be Grace of quiet words and demure dresses, but I'm going to ask for what I want and say no when I need to.

I'll play my music whenever and wherever I want. I might learn how to fight in the *ludus* or man the laser torpedos from the bridge. I can enjoy my feminine side, *and* be hard as nails. I like me just the way I am *and* I can create an even better me in the coming days.

And Tyree. He's grown to be a badass in his own right. He didn't just grow a hundred pounds of gorgeous muscle, he's become masculine in his thinking and desires and actions. His body's strong, and he's self-assured enough to be proud of exactly who he is.

He knows what he wants, and that's to love me and protect me and make me feel good not just in my body but in my soul. He calls us truemates. I call it love. No matter the name, we want the same thing—the rest of our lives together, roaming this galaxy in a lifetime of adventure.

Dear Reader

I hope you enjoyed <u>Tyree,</u> the third in the Galaxy Gladiator Series Keep reading to get a peek at Devolose's story, which is the next in the series. Trust me, by the end of his first chapter (below) you'll see there's much more to his story than met the eye in Tyree's book.

Want to know what initially made Shadow such an angsty jerk? Sign up for my free **newsletter** to read the FREE novelette with his backstory, Terminus: Shadow's Prequel My newsletter will be full of early peaks, cover releases, giveaways, extra content and other fun stuff.

You'll find lots of freebies on my store at www.shopalanak han.com See you there.

REQUEST FOR REVIEWS: Reviews equal love for an author, and also help us keep writing. You don't need to write a book report unless you want to, just a few sentences about what you liked (or didn't). I promise I read every single one.

Hugs,

Alana

Sneak Peek : Devolose

PRESENT DAY

Somewhere in Space on the Vessel *Leaf on the Wind* (formerly known as *Sweet Deliverance*)

Chapter One

Tawny

"I officially call this tribunal to order," Captain Zar intones solemnly. "A male's life hangs in the balance."

Every male and female aboard are crammed onto the bridge of this ship. There are twelve females, all abducted from Earth in the last few months and thrown together with twelve alien males from different species. The males, most of whom were gladiator slaves, overthrew their masters and stole this vessel. Now they're all on the run from their ruthless previous owners.

Of course, that doesn't include Devolose and me. This tribunal is being conducted to convict him of the crime of torturing and abusing me. He asked me, then forbade me, then begged me not to speak today. Fuck him. I'll talk if I want to.

"Since none of us males know the first thing about legal proceedings, we will follow Earth protocol." Zar was a slave as far back as he can remember. He's humanoid but looks feline, complete with fur, a tail, and facial features resembling a lion. He was voted captain after the rebellion and is presiding over this tribunal.

"Maddie will be acting as . . . let me consult my notes, Counsel for the Defense. Savannah will be . . . Prosecuting. I don't need to remind you to treat these proceedings with respect. You will all be voting after the evidence has been presented. Proceed."

A former Marine on Earth, Savannah's a pretty brunette with blunt-cut shoulder-length hair. She has no formal legal training; I guess she just watched a lot of legal shows on TV. It doesn't matter, by the firm set of her jaw and the angry look in her eyes, she's not going to cut Devolose any slack.

She steps to the front of the bridge, which has floor-to-ceiling windows over about eighty percent of the bullet-shaped room. "Ladies and gentlemen of the jury, I'm here to present evidence today to convict Devolose of crimes so serious I am asking for the death penalty. I will only be calling two witnesses. I will not be calling the victim, Tawny, as we've deemed her too fragile to give testimony."

Anger flares as I ball my fists at my sides. I want to object, but I catch Devolose's quelling, almost imperceptible frown. I'll bide my time—wait and see. I clamp my mouth shut, but I know everyone in the room can see me glower. Fragile my ass.

"I call Tyree to the stand," Savannah motions to the large first mate's swivel chair near the front of the room. He should be comfortable there; I'm told he's the first mate. He's a tall, muscular male wearing a loincloth. He's handsome and very humanoid, with tan skin and elongated elf-like ears.

He and his human mate, Grace, rescued Devi and me. Well, they rescued me—they didn't want to leave a fellow human in that awful dungeon. They only brought Devi along because I refused to leave planet Emirus without him.

"First, I would like to enter as fact that Tyree has the capability to see into people's minds. He exhibited this psychic ability when he helped coordinate our rebellion and crawled into our former captain's mind to get him to disable our pain/kill collars. Does anyone dispute this fact?"

Savannah looks around the room, waiting for an objection, but there is none. "With his clairvoyance entered into evidence, Tyree, can you tell us what you know about Devolose's crimes?"

She steps away so that everyone can focus on Tyree. I have no idea what he saw in the emperor's wicked mind, but first of all, I know it isn't going to be good for Devi, and second, I imagine it's going to embarrass the shit out of me.

"I snuck into the Emperor of Emirus' mind to see what we were up against when I thought he meant to do Grace and me harm. Many things I saw there were shocking. I will say I am very glad that man is dead." He pauses and looks at his mate, Grace; she's blushing.

I'm not sure everyone on board knows that Grace killed the emperor with a paring knife. She stabbed him until her arm was too tired to keep plunging the knife into his chest. I thank God every day she killed that motherfucker, and that I was lucky enough to watch the whole thing.

"Tyree, can you share what you observed that is pertinent to why we're here?" Savannah prompts in her serious, prosecutorial tone.

"I saw that man," he dramatically points at Devi as if he's seen a thousand episodes of *Law and Order*, "beat Tawny repeatedly. I saw him hit and abuse her all over her body. Even her . . . sexual areas."

My face heats, and even though I'm looking straight ahead at Devi, who's sitting in a chair toward the windows a few few fromTyree, I know every eye in the room is on me.

"I saw him slap and punch as well as use whips. I saw many episodes, over months if not *annums*. It occurred in the emperor's bedroom as well in the dungeon in the cell that devil," he points at Devolose again, "shared with that poor female."

He indicates me as if there is any doubt who the "poor female" in this room is.

"He was relentless. I saw the look on his face, heard him call her unspeakable names—he enjoyed what he was doing." He swallows hard, too upset to continue as he rubs his fist against his bronzed chest.

"Thank you." Savannah seems to take pity on him. "That will be all."

He rises and returns to one of the small jump seats ringing the rear of the room, five seats down from me. His mate Grace sits gently on his lap and lovingly slips her arm around the back of his neck.

I try to connect with Devi's gaze, but his eyes are unfocused, jaw muscle leaping in his otherwise emotionless face. Just observing him, you'd think he was watching a boring movie, not on trial for his life. I sneak a peek at some of the others in the room. If looks could kill, Devi would be dead already. I'm not feeling optimistic.

My heart is clenching. I don't want them to punish Devi for what he did. They all think I have Stockholm Syndrome. They're wrong.

"I now call Dr. Drayke sun Omrun to the stand," Savannah says.

The blue-skinned doctor in his dark blue jumpsuit sits stiffly in the designated chair. "Dr. Drayke, I understand you did a thorough examination on Tawny Britton, what were your findings?"

"Miss Tawny exhibited bruises and lacerations in every stage of healing. These findings are consistent with repeated, unrelenting abuse that went on regularly." He pauses and swallows as he wipes his palms on his thighs. I find myself mimicking that gesture to cope with my own anxiety.

I know what he's going to disclose next. I'm embarrassed and angry that all this personal information about me has to be disclosed to every being on this ship. How will I ever be able to look any of them in the eye? All they'll ever think about when they see me is what he's going to say next.

"There was . . . ample evidence of sadistic and repeated aggression against her . . . intimate areas. Both external and internal."

He glances at me, maybe a silent apology that he had to share that private information in such a public forum. Sorry doctor, apology <u>not</u> accepted. Ever hear of HIPAA? I wish *I* had psychic powers; I'd use them to set this entire ship on fire. Fuck them all. I'm not sure they care about me or my feelings. They just want to convict Devolose.

"One final question, doctor," Savannah says as if it's an after-thought. Uh oh, this can't be good.

"Did you ask Miss Britton how she received these injuries?"

"Yes."

"And her response?" Savannah prods.

"She said she received almost all of them at Devolose's hand."

"Thank you, doctor Drayke, I have no further questions. You may step down."

Savannah waits until all eyes are on her, then continues, "My closing remarks will be brief. I have presented evidence that the Defendant was observed inflicting these wounds on Miss Britton, that the abuse was ongoing and unremitting, that it damaged her seriously, and that by her own admission it was administered by the Defendant. I rest my case."

Devolose

I told my defense attorney Maddie I did not want this *dracking* trial. I knew it would bring deep shame to Tawny. I'm certain no one else can read her like I can. After three *annums* in a cell together, I know every nuance of emotion her sweet face is capable of.

Her eyes are sad and downcast—it's obvious she's embarrassed. As well she should be; all these people shouldn't be privy to these intimate details of her abuse. It's not proper. And she's angry, too. Her jaw is tight. I didn't want this trial because I didn't want any more shame to fall upon her.

I asked Maddie to tell the captain I didn't want a tribunal. I admitted every act, in far more detail than was shared in this room today. I should be put to death. Throw me out the garbage jettison and let me die in the cold silence of space. The captain refused.

Maddie walks to the front of the room. We met twice before today; she said it was to prepare my defense. Her brown curls are loose in a wild tangle around her face. It doesn't matter what she looks like; there's nothing she can say to the jury to help my case. I've given her no evidence to help her defend me. I deserve no defense.

"Ladies and gentlemen of the jury, Captain Zar, umm . . . I have no evidence to present." She shrugs her shoulders and turns to Zar and adds in a low tone, "He told me nothing that would help his case."

"He said nothing?" Zar asks.

She shakes her head, "Nothing in his own defense."

She approaches him and whispers. Perhaps she's only now telling him I admitted everything and asked to be put to death.

"He told you that?"

"Yes."

"Maddie, I think you need to ask him to say that now, during the trial," Zar states firmly.

"On Earth, people can't be forced to testify against themselves." Maddie bites her lip, her shoulders hunched. Perhaps she feels bad that she hasn't properly done her job. I'll save her some misery.

I stand and address the males and females who are going to determine my fate. Most, including Tawny, are in small seats up against the back wall of this space. "Every mark and every bruise you see on Tawny's skin was administered by me. She did not deserve even one of those. As the doctor testified, I performed those actions repeatedly and over time. I agree I should be put to death." There is no emotion in my voice because I am emotionless. Tyree called me a devil. He's correct.

Tawny's fidgeting in her seat and spearing me with a look that could kill me where I stand. I know she's mad I won't say anything in my defense.

She wants to speak on my behalf, but what can she say? The females came to my cell on board this vessel—the one she insists on sharing with me. They told her about Stockholm Syndrome; they said she has it because she doesn't want to leave my side. They're right. She'll be better off with me dead. It will allow her to move on with her life and forget what happened every day in that dungeon for three miserable *annums.*

Tawny

Everyone on the jury is murmuring to each other. This trial is now officially a farce. Really, what verdict could they possibly return? There's no evidence that would point to anything other than a conviction.

"Can we vote?" a tall, muscular, Neanderthal-looking male asks. He looks mad enough to strangle Devi with his bare hands—and big enough to accomplish it.

I've been locked in a cell in the bowels of this ship since we were brought on board five days ago. To everyone's credit they offered me a nice cabin near all the other Earth women, but I refused--I didn't want to be separated from Devolose. I only know a few of these people. Of course, now they know more about me than anyone has a right to know.

"You should have time to discuss this among yourselves," Maddie protests.

"I think we all know the verdict already," one of the women answers contemptuously.

I stand up and raise my voice over all their chatter, "I'd like to speak!"

Devi stands up and yells, "No!" It's the first time he's shown any emotion to the jury.

Zar rises, commanding silence with his presence and demeanor. "Tawny, we wanted to protect you from this. The females say you have some sickness that's made you care about your abuser."

Devi's staring lasers through me—I know he doesn't want me to talk. Well, fuck it. I don't care if there's not one person in this room who wants to hear what I have to say—I need to say it. All these males are huge and intimidating; I don't give a crap. Everyone has decided I'm "sick" and not entitled to a voice. Screw it.

I walk forward and stand on a chair facing the jury, Devi at my back. I raise my hands for quiet and forge ahead. "I don't care whether you all think I deserve to be heard or not. I'm going to say my piece no matter what you want." I toss my head over my shoulder and snap, "You, too, Devi.

"Despite the fact that the defendant wants to be pushed out the garbage chute, there actually *is* another side to this story."

"Devolose was a slave, just as I was. He was a slave before I got there. He tells me he served not only this emperor but his father and his grandfather. He was forced to do their bidding, just as anyone in this room who was a slave was forced to do the bidding of their master.

"The emperor was a madman, let's all agree to that. What Devi's master had him do was . . . horrific. My injuries tell the tale of just how horrific." I take a deep breath to quiet my nerves. Everyone in the room is paying attention now, and their stares make me so anxious I cross my arms in front of my chest as if to protect myself.

"What you don't know, and what Tyree's psychic images didn't tell you, was how much it distressed Devi to do what he did. What Tyree couldn't know was that Devi became a master at sleight of hand. He learned to make each blow, each crack of the whip, sound and look worse than it was. Did it still hurt? Yes. Did it still damage my body and my soul? Absolutely. But Devi tried his hardest to lessen the pain.

"Did you see pleasure in Devi's face as he hit me, Tyree? I'm certain you did because Devi became an actor to convince the emperor he was beating the shit out of me and enjoying it.

"Did you hear Devi call me a bitch and a whore and tell me I deserved it, Tyree? Of course you did, because it kept the emperor fired up and distracted from the fact that some of the blows didn't even touch my flesh.

"Did you see Devi and me practice in the dungeon under covers late at night? He taught me how to keep my hands to one side and clap when he pretended to smack me. It made such a convincing sound, a blow didn't even have to land on me.

"Did you see all that Tyree? Or just what you wanted to see?

"Why didn't Devi defy the emperor? You met the emperor, Tyree. He would have killed Devi in a heartbeat, and the new taskmaster would have hurt me a hundred times worse. Do you have any idea how many times I heard Devi's muted prayers at night, begging his God to kill him in his sleep? But he stayed around. To protect me.

"Did you notice that when we were forced to bed down together, every single night he put his lips to my ear and apologized for what he'd been forced to do during the day? He stole salve at his own peril and administered it to me when my wounds became infected. He told me stories to take my mind off the terror of every day and every minute of my life. And he told me," I turn my head and look straight at him accusingly, "that he would take care of me if we ever escaped that dungeon."

Tears spill from my eyes as I pierce him with my gaze. "You promised, Devi. You promised to take care of me after our escape. I want to hold you to that."

I look at Zar and then every member of the jury in turn. "Devi has suffered enough. Every blow he administered to me hurt him as well. He deserves a chance at a life. And I deserve to share it with him."

I stop and grab a deep breath. I take stock of the jury, and I'm not sure they're convinced. The next thing I'm about to say will piss Devi off to the point he might never want to speak to me again if he is released, but I believe it will save his life. I have to say it.

"Doctor Drayke." I look at him directly. "Can you testify as to what you observed when you examined Devolose?"

"No!" Devi shouts from behind me. "No! I forbid it. Just kill me. I don't need to be humiliated as well."

The doctor stands, looking at Zar for direction.

"Answer the question," Zar instructs.

Devi groans. I glance behind me and see him slump forward, his hands covering his face.

The doctor's face is tight, his lips in a thin line as he reports, "He carries the marks of repeated and persistent beatings, whippings, and cuts."

I hear Devi sigh in relief behind me, but I've got to be relentless if I'm going to save his life.

"I believe you're leaving out a significant detail, Dr. Drayke." I wait, knowing the doctor will eventually fill the silence with the information the jury needs to hear.

"His penis has been fully amputated from his body." The doctor's lips thin into a line, then he dips his head and takes his seat.

There were a lot of shocked gasps and now it's silent in our little courthouse.

"Almost everyone in here has worn a pain/kill collar," I say. "Can I ask everyone here to stand?" I wait until every male and female in the room is standing—except for Devi. "Is there anyone in this room who has not done something they regret, something they're sorry for, something that went against everything they thought they stood for when they were threatened with pain or death? Please take a seat if you've never been forced to do something you didn't want to do."

No one. Not one being in this room sits.

"Your honor, I rest my case."

Continue reading DEVOLOSE here.

About Alana Khan

Alana Khan is a Pinnacle Award-winning, USA TODAY Best-selling author whose pen traverses galaxies and explores the extraordinary.

In a life as diverse as her stories, Alana boasts IMDB film credits, thrilling Harley adventures on open roads, and a stint as a professional spoon player—because, why not?

With a background as a psychotherapist, she delves into the human psyche, enriching her storytelling.

Join her on fantastical journeys through her novels, where cosmic romance and monstrous love merge with spice as hot as a Carolina Reaper chili pepper.

Want to read the next books in the series? Check out Alana's other books? Help yourself to 15% off anything in the store including dozens of $5.99 audios.

Go to my website for FREE books at
http://www.alanakhan.com/

My Shopify Store

Website:

Bookbub:

Goodreads:

Twitter:

Facebook:

Allmylinks:

Amazon Author Page:

Discover my channel on YouTube:

Want more of my books?

keep the lights on, there is plenty of action, romance, and steam.

Galaxy Warriors Alien Abduction Romance Series

What was I thinking writing 19 books in the Galaxy Gladiators series? Call it temporary insanity. This series is similar to Gladiators, but lets new readers jump in without knowing any backstory. Action, adventure, my trademark spice, and romance.

Galaxy Games Hostile Planet Alien Romance Series

All the heart-pounding passion and gut-clenching action I could cram onto the page. This series will grab you by the throat from the first page and never let you go. More action and hotter than previous series. And love. Did I forget to mention love?

Awakened from the Ice Series

In a world where the past and present collide, the Awakened From the Ice series brings ancient Rome roaring into the 21st century. When a group of Roman gladiators, perfectly preserved in ice, are discovered and revived, the course of history is forever altered.

This series offers a unique blend of historical insight, futuristic technology, and timeless romance. With each awakening, new challenges arise, testing the bonds of friendship, loyalty, and love. Immerse yourself in this thrilling saga where ancient valor meets modern courage, and love proves to be the ultimate force of nature.

Rescued by the Monsters Reverse Harem Romance series

In a future dystopian Earth, males have been spliced with animal DNA. Human women have been reduced to chattel and when they say no, even once, they're banished Down Below to where the "monsters" live. This series will soon have you wondering just who the monsters are as the human women each bond with three adoring human/animal hybrids.

Wolven Warriors Series

In a world where fantasy meets the modern age, a pack of otherworldly protectors called the Wolven Warriors walks among us. These humanoid males, with their wolf-like features, dropped to Earth 25 years ago. Discover a captivating modern-day fantasy where romance ignites amidst danger, and the Wolven Warriors must fight not only for survival but for the forbidden love that binds them to their human soulmates.

Arixxia Fields: A Steamy Small-Town Alien Romance Series

Are you ready to party? I imagine so, after reading all the drama in all my previous series. Each of these books is short, sexy, romantic, and FUN. Each revolves around a holiday. Check them out.

Hybrid Hearts Series

Bred to be soldiers, these rescued genetically engineered males are all given a new lease on life. How does the United States military plan to do that? They create an isolated town with cute shops and train the males in new jobs. How about a sexy lion-man baker for starters?

Galaxy Artificials Series

Packed with passion and spice, USA TODAY Bestselling author Alana Khan brings robots to life in this science fiction romance series. Oh yeah, she manages to give the metallic buckets of bolts smokin' hot humanoid bodies, too.

Orcfire Series

Twenty-five years ago, thousands of Others (orcs, nagas, minotaurs, and other species only known in fairytales) fell onto the burning sands of the Mojave Desert with no way to go home. They were rounded up by the U.S. Military and placed in a fenced enclosure on the outskirts of Los Angeles. The OrcFire series features one hot, green, tusked orc as the hero of each book as they battle fires and so much more to find their happily ever after. The OrcFire series will be hot, hot, hot in all ways.

Treasured by the Zinn Alien Abduction Romance Series

The US government gave the Zinns permission to take human women as wives. Let's just say the unsuspecting women, who know nothing of this unsavory deal, are none too happy–until they fall in love.

Mastered by the Zinn Alien Abduction Romance Series

Welcome to the enticing universe of 'Mastered by the Zinn,' a secret arrangement that's endured for centuries. The government's shadowy pact with the alien Zinn species allows for the abduction of human women in exchange for cutting-edge military technology. It's a clandestine game of risk and reward, desire and dominance.